RESTRICTED
FANTASIES

BY KEVIN KNEUPPER

CONTENTS

SEVEN MINUTES IN HEAVEN

JUST ONE MORE TIME.

I pull the helmet from my head, fastening it back into place at the top of my chair. I unplug the data cables from my arm, carefully twisting them out of the ports implanted in my wrist. Then I swivel back to the holographic display. It curves around me, floating in the air over my workstation.

Well, not *my* workstation. Temporary Labor Position #373867. But it was the one I sat down at yesterday afternoon, and by now it feels like it's mine.

I could go home if I wanted to. I can always go home. It's not like I need to work. It's not like anybody does. I get a monthly deposit into my account just like everybody else, minus ninety-five percent for my Total Goods and Services Plan. Enough to live a pretty happy life. No frills or anything, but I could just sit there and be happy if that's what I wanted.

But it's not what I want. I want to work. I love it more than anything.

It's not the place. The building's drab, and the walls are grey inside and out. The only decorations here are posters of the President. Not the President President, but the President of SocialCorp. Not that it matters. He's the more important one these days. He smiles down at us from every angle, his skin a porcelain white, his hair still lush and full. It's greying at the temples a bit, but he's still the man he always was.

We all heard the legends as kids. SocialCorp makes sure everybody knows and everybody hears. There were always new cartoon vids popping into the feed on my Pad, telling and retelling the stories. The history of how SocialCorp was made. About the old culture, the bad culture, the one he got rid of. How he realized that if it wasn't on the feeds, then nobody saw it anyway. How he freed us from the way we used to live and built us a brand new culture from scratch. A cleaner one, a better one, a less divisive one. Control the feeds and you control the kids, says the President. Control the kids and you control the culture, and he knows what he's talking about. He's given us everything we have.

I've been here maybe thirty-four hours, so it'll be time to leave soon. Just one more time and I'll leave. I stand and stretch. I'm a little cramped, so I flick my hands with a quick motion. The hologram inches upward in response. It'll be another two, maybe three hours, and this time I'll stand while I work.

A servobot hustles by. It looks like a little white pillar about three feet high, wheels at its base and a tray on the top. It's covered with the essentials: odor zappers, breath pills, amphetamines, and razors. I skip the amphetamines; this won't be an all-nighter. Not two in a row. I grab a FizzyCaff instead, pop it open, and then I'm ready to go.

I poke my finger at the hologram and the feeds start flowing. Where it all comes from, I couldn't even guess. Some bot somewhere flagged it all for human review, pics and vids and chatter that looked like BadPosts. The bots aren't smart enough to tell. They need us for that. Curators.

They flow across the display, one after the other. "My cat is such a little bitch," says the first, and it goes on and on. I don't read the rest. Racy, but not so bad as to justify a flag. I swipe it green and it's on to the next. A vid of a guy getting hit in the nuts. You can see some skin, but not too much. Swipe green, then the next vid, then the next.

There's a meter on the right of my screen, rising from the bottom to the top. I've barely made a dent in it: a few thousand points, and I'm gonna need a million. But with each swipe, I get a little closer. A picture of a treasure chest pops open each time I finish reviewing a post, and a number bursts out with what I've won. Ten points sometimes, sometimes a hundred. If luck's with me it could even be a few thousand. Closer and closer to the goal every time I swipe. It draws me in, and once I've started I can't quit. I can't even take a break to piss. I mean I can, but I don't want to, and there's a servobot designed to take care of that if I really need it.

I'm at about 45,000 points when I hit my first HatePost. The feeds have to be kept clean. Sanitized. A culture gets sick when you let the sick stuff in. The President says so, and he's the one who'd know. It's hidden inside a six-minute long vid of a dog chasing around a beaver. At the three minute mark, it all changes.

A pic flashes across the screen: an image of Asia from space, grey mist swirling across the entire continent. "The Great Smog of China," it says in big red letters. Then a city covered in sickly yellow clouds and a flash of text: "Climate Change Cover-Up to Juke Profit Numbers! Major Corps demand strict air regs at home, then send our factories to the Greater PRC where regs are a joke! Search for pics of 'chinese air pollution' on FreeCrawl and you'll see…."

A HatePost. If you let that stuff into your feeds, the network splits apart. A culture can't maintain itself if you let in the voices of hate. You have to know the same things, read the same things, believe the same things. Otherwise you're not a culture. You're a company at war with itself, and a company can't take care of its people if they're busy fighting one another.

I swipe red as quickly as I can, averting my eyes so I don't see any more than I have to. Whoever posted the vid's going to get a flag on their account, and I'm not risking one on mine. They'll get docked some of their basic income for sure, even if they didn't know that stuff was in there. Most people don't; they just repost the vid without watching it all the way through. It's still an infraction. The company's tracking my eyes, and it knows what part of the screen I'm looking at. If I take too long to look away, I might get flagged for Problematic Behavior. I'd lose points for that, tens of thousands of them.

And I need points. More than anything else, I need my points.

I keep curating the feeds, keep swiping red and green. The treasure chest explodes each time, and each time I feel an eager anticipation, then a little glow of warmth inside when I see how many I've earned.

A million. A million's all I need, and then I'll be done for the day. My eyes are so bleary I can barely even see. I couldn't keep myself awake if it weren't for that little treasure chest. It drives me. It drags me in. I'm at half a million, so close to the goal. My body's yelling at me to sleep, but not just yet. I can make it there. The points come every twenty or thirty seconds, and every time they do it's like a little burst of focus. A hit of dopamine, the good stuff, pure and uncut.

Next up is a vid with a subtle pitch in the middle for an out-company cleaning product. I mark it HatePost; that's how they seduce you. Get that one little sale, and pretty soon you're signing a contract with another corp and they're the one entitled to your basic minimum from the government. If you leave the corp, you leave the culture. You leave the family. You leave your friends, and you leave them forever. That's what the President says, right there in the Little Blue Book.

A political cartoon about the President. HatePost for sure, and it's a big one. Five thousand points for catching that. Then a woman asking for help sending a message to her daughter, a subscriber of another corp. Not technically a HatePost, but it's Problematic regardless. Talk to people outside the company, and you risk infecting the corporate culture with something dangerous.

I flag it, and she'll probably get a good talking to even if they don't dock her monthly check. They'll be watching her for sure. Biological families tend to subscribe to a Total Goods and Services plan from the same company, but when there's a split, there's a high risk of a cancelled subscription. A stupid move if you do it before the contract term, because the company's entitled to your check until the very end. How the hell are you going to live for a year without a home, without health care, without food, without everything the company gives you?

It's just not worth it. The company's usually a better family than the one you were born with anyway. And then there's the matter of the points. You'd lose your points, and you'd lose your progress, lose everything you'd spent all those hours working for. You'd be starting from scratch, right from the bottom. And that's a hell of a thing to do.

I swipe and swipe and swipe. The time flies by; I glance at the clock, and it's been around two hours. I didn't even notice. It felt like it was only a few minutes with all the points I've been earning. I'm pushing myself so far I don't even hear anything around me. It's like my peripheral vision is gone. All that's left is the screen. The swiping and the points. More than anything else, the points.

And then it happens. The number creeps upward. I'm nearly there. 991,663.

So, so close.

I was tiring out, but I get a second wind. I flag a servobot and down another FizzyCaff.

992,787.

I keep swiping. I'm perked up again, the prospect of hitting a million giving me back all my energy, all my drive. At 995,000 I wave over another servobot, this time to take a quick piss. I don't even move. A little tube snakes up my pants and after a minute or so I'm done. I've got to get ready. I don't want to have to go when the number flips over a million.

997,335.

998,642.

I'm so close.

I'm buzzing with anticipation. My leg's tapping up and down. I'm leaning forward in my seat. I can't wait. I just can't.

And then a last HatePost puts me over the line. I catch a guy downvoting a picture of the President, and the treasure chest burps open. 2,000 points. Just enough to get my million.

I jump to my feet, pumping my fist in the air. There's a muted "grats" from the nearby cubicles. There's people there, but I don't know any of them. We say hi sometimes, but that's not what we're here for. We didn't come here to talk.

We came here to play.

A pair of servobots hum towards me. I sit back down in my chair. They switch out the cables in my arms, jacking me into an entirely different system. When they're done, I reach up towards the helmet on the top of my chair. I fasten it on, pull the visor over my eyes, and I can feel the servobots hooking it up to a port in my neck.

And then I'm not there anymore.

I'm back in the game. A dragon's in front of me, big and scaly and mean. Fangs a foot long, sharp ridges running along his back, tufts of smoke snorting out of his nostrils. He's killed me three times, but this time he's mine. I look down at my body: muscular, sinewy, the physique of a barbarian. I've got the sword to match, strapped to my back. I pull it out and take a pose.

6 minutes and 30 seconds left.

I drink some potions. Fireproof my skin, put up a magic shield, buff all my stats. A bar shows up in the corner of my vision, showing me how strong I am, how tough I am, how much damage I can take. I'm ready.

6 minutes.

I charge towards the dragon. His head lunges at me. I somersault forward, his jaws snapping into the ground and missing me by inches. I pivot, thrusting my sword up into his neck. It's a hit: blood splurts down onto me, warm liquid goo against my skin. I can smell his breath from here, an acrid sulfur stench that makes me want to retch.

But I don't. I'm a warrior. I cling to my sword, tearing through the dragon's flesh. I've got him in a weak spot, and if I can pull a little harder, I'll rip his throat clean out. But he's not going down that easily. He rears back, lifting his head up into the air. I hold onto the sword for dear life. My body weight's doing the work for me, cutting a gash down his neck. He claws at me, but his stubby little arms can't quite reach. Then he starts shaking like a wet dog, hurling me this way and that until finally I can't hold on anymore.

3 minutes.

I'm thrown to the ground. No sword, no weapon. I toss a rock at him. Doesn't do a thing. I'm running, zig-zagging around the field of battle. Blasts of fire nip at my toes. I get hit on the leg: the skin's scorched, but I don't feel any pain. Just a light rumbling feeling that lets me know I've taken some damage. I see my health bar dropping in the corner of my eyes. He hits me again, dead in the chest. Another rumble, and now my skin looks roasted. It's the same way he got me last time. Another one like that and I'm done.

2 minutes.

One last chance. I charge towards him, digging into his scales with my fingers. I climb up his leg. He's shaking, howling, spraying fire. I make it to his back. I'm holding on for dear life, but all I'm paying attention to is my sword, stained red and sticking out of his neck. I wait for my moment. And then I jump.

My hands hit the sword. I've got it. The force of it pulls me down, and it rips him wide open. He tries to scream, but his vocal cords are shot from the wound. He stumbles, then collapses, and I roll away from the corpse and onto the ground.

1 minute.

There's a treasure chest behind him. There's always a treasure chest. I sprint towards it. Put a hand on it. And like magic, it flips open.

An ancient axe. Enchanted boots. A crapload of gold. And now I'm maybe one more kill away from another level.

10 seconds.

No time for anything else. I bask in the adrenaline rush, running a finger along my shiny new axe, trying on the boots and checking out how I look. The design's amazing, they've got these little skulls on the sides, way cooler than what I was wearing before—

And then it all goes black.

I can hear the servobots whining as they unplug me and lift off the helmet. I'm back in my cubicle. Back in my life. No more sword, no more monsters, and no more adventures. I'm done for now. I'm beat. I've been at this for a full day straight, and I'm about to collapse. All I want to do is go home, go to bed, and get a good night's rest.

I'm gathering up my things. There's a post up on the screen: a frowny face next to an article about recent cuts to the basic minimum income. Clearly a HatePost, clearly Problematic. What the hell? I flag it as both; it'd be stupid not to. I knew I'd get a bonus for flagging it, and boy did I: five thousand points. I feel a little surge of happiness, and I get a little energy back.

I know I've been here forever. But it's not that long in the scheme of things. I've done four days in a row before, one time almost five. I swipe another post, and then another. Just one more. Just another few thousand points. I'm thinking about those boots, about what I'm going to do next when I get back into the game. One more kill and I'll hit the next level. I can do that in seven minutes, easy. Another million points and I'll earn another seven minutes of play. I could be there in another hour, maybe two.

An hour's not that long. And besides, it's good for the company. Good for our culture. I keep swiping. Just a few more. It feels so good every time that treasure chest opens up. I'm not so sure I want to go home anymore. Not just yet. Maybe I'll stay that extra hour. Just get to the next level, and then I'll be done. It's not that big a deal. I'll go to sleep right after. Just get back in there, kill one more monster, and then I'm going home.

I wave over one of the servobots. This time I take the amphetamines. It'll make things a lot easier. I pop the pills, wash them down with another FizzyCaff, and turn back to my screen.

Then I swipe and I swipe and I swipe....

RESTRICTED FANTASIES

ONE MAN'S DREAM is another man's nightmare. I know that better than anybody. But it still surprises me, the things people fantasize about. There's some twisted minds out there, and some twisted ways to live.

Most people have dark dreams sometimes, and I get that. Lots of us even act them out. But some people go too far, and that's when I've got to step in. This one was awful enough that it made me want to vomit.

But at the end of the day, it was all just zeros and ones conjured from the depths of a very disturbed mind. A simulated reality tailored to someone else's wildest fantasies. None of it was real, no matter how much it might have felt like it was. I had to keep reminding myself of that if I wanted to get through it.

I knew what I was in for the moment I showed up at the outskirts of the city. It was ringed with a fifteen-foot concrete perimeter, an urban fortress walled away to protect it from enemies that didn't even exist. Every few yards were those banners. They ran the length of the wall from top to bottom, bloody red except for the swastikas at the center. And it only got worse once the guards waved me through the gate.

It started with the corpses, strung up on each and every lamp pole, dangling slowly in the wind. They'd been left to fester, puffy and bloated, hung there and forgotten like off-season Christmas lights. There were notes pinned to their chests, and I read a few of them as I walked along the street towards the city center. "Slav." "Gypsy." "Jew." He wasn't subtle, the man I'd come to see. And he was every bit as awful as the man he most admired.

The concentration camps were next, the barracks lined up one after another on either side of the road. I didn't catch much of them before I decided to just cover my eyes and stare down at the gravel in front of me. It was the people that got to me. They were watching me, fingers poking out through the chain-link fence. Men, women, and children, all of them thin as skeletons, moaning and wailing and begging me to do something. Begging me to save them, or if I couldn't, for just a little crust of bread to eat. Or something to drink. Even a drop. They'd do anything for a single drop.

I could cover my eyes, but I couldn't keep myself from hearing them. And I couldn't do anything about the stench. Burnt flesh mixed with a foul chemical stew. A waft of bleach, or something that smelled like it, and the odor of dirt-caked people who hadn't bathed in months. It sent me into a coughing fit, and I had to take off my suit jacket and cover up my nose just to get past them.

I kept telling myself that none of it was real, repeating it under my breath like a mantra. It was all just somebody else's fantasy, his own private world where he could live exactly how he pleased. That was the only way I was going to make it: reminding myself that none of it was real in the end.

But the longer I walked, the more I hated him for his fantasies. He'd put them here, right out in the front as a greeting to visitors. I expect he didn't get many. He wanted to offend me, to force me to run this gauntlet of horrors if I was going to see him. He didn't want me there, but he wasn't going to get rid of me that easily.

I came to a grassy plaza surrounded by a scattering of squat grey buildings. It was plastered with more banners, flapping those nasty lines back and forth in the wind. I could hear the speeches droning out over the city through the loudspeakers, chanting a never-ending prayer to false gods the rest of us had buried long ago. And there were more bodies hanging from the gallows in the center of the plaza, sacrificial tributes to the man they worshipped here.

A platoon of soldiers stomped through the streets in their metal helmets and their jackboots. A few of them pulled a frightened man into an alley. He was thin, with frizzy black hair tucked under his cap and hollow eyes filled with fear. "Jew," they said, and spat in his face. They shouted things at him, screaming into his ears from either side. One of them slapped him, knocking his cap to the ground.

"I'm not," he said. "My mother—"

The soldiers didn't care, and they didn't listen. They started into him, fists and elbows and knees barraging the man until his face was a featureless purple mush. He fell to the ground and they kept at it, kicking at his skull with their jackboots until the alley was covered in a sickly pink puddle and the man moved no more. They laughed, then, leaning against the alley wall to smoke their cigarettes and stare at me with predator's eyes as I passed.

All those things were bad, and all of them made my stomach turn. But they weren't the worst thing about the place, not by a longshot.

The worst thing was what he was doing to his kids.

I headed for a blocky concrete building that took up most of the city's center. It looked like a bunker, with barbed wire ringing the perimeter and rolling along the roof like a crown of thorns. The guards practically growled as I walked inside, but there was nothing they could do to me. I was real and they weren't, and their master knew he had to let me through. He didn't know why I was here, not yet, and he was probably hoping he could bluster his way past whatever bureaucratic obstacle I posed.

The inside of the building was all soldiers and checkpoints, cold efficiency without even a splotch of color to humanize the place. The guards pointed me towards a corner office at the end of the hall, and then they went back to their vigil. I walked there alone, opening the door and steeling myself for the confrontation to come. A man sat before me, the vision of Nordic perfection.

Heinrich Hesselmann.

His hair was blonde, his eyes were blue, and his skin had practically been bleached. He had the physique of an Olympian, even though he hadn't earned it.

I knew what he really looked like. I had photos, and they weren't anything like this. Potbellied and bald, with yellow teeth in place of yellow hair. Heinrich wasn't his real name, either. He'd been born as Bert Hamilton, but he didn't like the ring of that one. Not that any of it mattered. He was the one I'd come for, and the digital makeover couldn't hide who he really was. Not from me.

The walls of his office were lined with standards, golden eagles perching atop that flag he loved so much. A copy of Mein Kampf was on his desk, right there in the middle of it. He'd put it there to tweak me, I think. He didn't strike me as the type who liked to read. Heinrich's portrait took up most of the wall behind him, the idealized blonde version of him, his hand angled upwards in salute. Two soldiers stood at attention on either side of the door. Waffen-SS, by the uniforms. Those black jackets, those skulls, and the Iron Cross hanging from each of their necks. I knew exactly who they were, and I knew exactly who old Bert was, too.

"Mr. Hamilton," I said, extending my hand. His face went sour as I dropped his real name. Two could play these little games, and I was as happy to take jabs at him as he was to take them at me.

"Hesselmann," said Heinrich, bristling. "My name is Hesselmann."

"Nice place," I said. "Scenic."

"I thought you'd like it," said Heinrich. He muttered something under his breath. A command to the computer that ran the simulation, most likely. The speeches outside grew louder, angry German ravings that pounded against the walls of the building. I could hear a crowd in the square outside, warped into existence from

15

nowhere. They were applauding the speech, sounding out their salutes and roaring at every word.

But I couldn't let Heinrich rattle me. He wanted me scared, and he wanted me gone, and I wasn't going to give him the satisfaction.

"I expect you want to know why I'm here," I said.

"I already know," said Heinrich. "Because your Jew paymasters sent you. They gave you a handful of shekels to turn Judas against your own kind. They may run the world out there. But I run the world in here. And there isn't a damned thing you can do about it."

I didn't take the bait. I took a breath instead, kept my calm demeanor, and stayed professional for as long as I could manage it.

"You know the law, Heinrich," I said. "And you're breaking it."

"My world," said Heinrich. "My reality. My laws."

"To a point," I said. "But there's laws outside, too."

"I know the laws outside pretty damned well," said Heinrich. "And I've got a right to fantasize about whatever I want, period. Supreme Court says so. I take it you've heard of *Wheeler v. Quarterman*?" I had, of course. A seminal legal case, the one that made all of this possible. He smiled smugly, savoring a victory he thought was already in the bag. "My fantasies are private, and so are everyone else's. The law says you can't regulate what I do in here. Don't like it? Get your own simulation."

I hated when they got like this. They always did when they cut themselves off from everyone else for long enough. He was right, in a sense. This was his reality. He was the ruler of his own private kingdom, a virtual reality world that he could run however he pleased. The law was clear on that: a person's private fantasies are their own private business.

It had taken a while to get there. We'd tried regulation at first, but that was a mess. Too many weirdos, too many people to go after, and too many people who thought they were the normal ones and everyone else's fantasies should be banned instead. And after the Great Social Media War of 2037, nobody was interested in another ten or twenty thousand deaths over somebody else's political views, no matter extreme they were. The courts had stepped in and ruled that regulating what someone does in the privacy of their own simulation was entirely unconstitutional, the violence had finally stopped, and that was that.

But the law Heinrich was hiding behind wasn't the only law. He'd crossed a line. He was a grown man, and he could simulate whatever fantasies he wanted.

His children were an entirely different matter.

I cleared my throat, and then I started into it. The reason I'd come to this bleak little place, this throwback to a world most people just wanted to forget about. "This environment. It's inappropriate. Kids shouldn't be raised in it. You know better than that."

Heinrich's eyes narrowed, and his perfect face was marred with a scowl. He hadn't seen that one coming. He'd thought I was just some helpless bureaucrat here to put a scare into him. It happened from time to time, when the craziest ones left their sims and started trying to force their reality onto everyone else. He'd thought I didn't know what he'd done, and he'd thought he was safe. Now his eyes lit with suspicion. "They're my kids.

My family. And it's our right to live however we please."

"That's true enough for you," I said. "But not for them."

"Go to hell," snarled Heinrich. "Or better yet, go right on down to the camps. We've still got them, just up the road." I must have squirmed a little in the chair. His mouth curved up into half a smirk, his tongue flicking out and lapping up my discomfort. "You can smell 'em from here, if you open up the window. Thousands and thousands of Jews, burning away into ash. Just like they did in the forties. Just like they should have done to all of 'em."

I didn't react, and I didn't let him get to me. I just snapped my fingers and my business card appeared in my hand, materializing from nowhere. I flipped the card onto his desk with a theatrical toss, and his eyes went cold as he read it: Mark Kenneton, Department of Social Services, Restricted Fantasies Division.

It was a little trick I had to let them know I meant business. Some of them thought they could control everything as long as it was inside their own sim. They were right, to a point, but we had a few tools of our own. "I saw what you're simulating. I saw it all. Fine for you, but your kids are minors, and I make the rules for them. And I say this little sim of yours is an entirely inappropriate environment to raise children in."

He rolled the card in his hands, memorizing my name. Probably thought he'd retaliate somehow, or tell one of his real world buddies about me and ask them to threaten me offline. I wasn't scared. Not a bit. There were thousands of men just like him. They lived in private fantasy worlds, simulations of history gone wrong. Worlds where the Germans had won the war and everything was the way it should have been, if only the Führer had gotten his way.

But having thousands of men behind you didn't matter if every one of them was a coward. They could talk a big game inside their sims, but none of them would ever leave their VR pods to confront you in real life. They certainly wouldn't do it to fight someone else's battle, not even for someone like Heinrich who was one of their own.

"You say this place is inappropriate for children," said Heinrich. "What about your world? Run by Jews. Filled with mongrels, with Aryans made slaves to the lesser races. My kids won't be raised in a place like that. They're going to grow up here. With me. With the world like it's supposed to be."

"They're not just your kids," I said. "I talked to your wife. And she's not exactly happy about this."

Unhappy was an understatement. She'd been hysterical, and if she hadn't turned us onto Heinrich we'd probably have never even known what he was doing. Two daughters, and he'd kidnapped them both. He'd taken them on a routine custody visit, and then he'd just disappeared. It'd been years before we'd been able to track any of them down, and even then we'd only managed to find Heinrich. Where his daughters were was anyone's guess.

"She's a bitch," said Heinrich. He made a cutting gesture across his throat with one of his fingers. "A bitch and a snitch."

I'd met guys like this before. My mom married one of them a few years after she broke up with my dad. I spent my teenage years being raised in-sim, and it wasn't any more pleasant than what Heinrich was doing to his own kids. My dad still got visitation, and every day he had us was a risk. They never knew what I was going to say to him, and they never knew what ideas I'd come back to the sim with.

My mother's new husband didn't like me going, and he did everything he could to stop me. And any time he even suspected that I'd said a word about how we lived to anyone outside of the family, I caught a beating, or worse. You could do terrible things to someone in-sim, and none of it would ever leave a mark. Snitches got stitches. That's what he always said. You needed to teach your kids that attitude if they were going to keep something like this a secret for very long.

"You'll never find them," said Heinrich. "Never in a million years. You can look and look and look. They might not even be in the country." His face lit up with a triumphant glow. "I know I'm not."

"Bangkok Smiles and Happiness Simulation Center," I said. "We looked." The really screwed up types tended to end up in places like that. It was easier to find someone willing to design the type of sim you wanted to live in, no questions asked. And there wasn't any risk of the place that was housing you suddenly growing a conscience and deleting all of your code.

"They could be here, too," said Heinrich. "There isn't any extradition from here, not for crimes in-sim. They could be anywhere. The world's too big. Too many pods to search. Billions and billions."

He was right, about the real world at least. Billions of people living out their lives in whatever private fantasy they wanted. Most of them stay connected with the rest of society, even if only virtually. Normal people keep their sex fantasies to themselves and spend the rest of their time in the multis. You can talk with people in the multis, and you're all playing in the same sandbox.

But the crazy ones, they live alone. They have to, because most of them fantasize about shitting all over everyone who isn't exactly like them. I've seen some screwed up stuff. I've seen fantasies about killing off all the men or enslaving all the women. I've seen fantasies for every race, color, or creed where one of them rules over all the other ones. And I once saw a fantasy about "social justice" where everyone had to correctly use 1,187 different personal pronouns on penalty of death.

This Nazi thing wasn't the darkest fantasy I'd come across, not by a longshot. The world my mother's husband put me into was even worse. And every political group had its crazies, even if one particular side can only ever see the crazies on the other. Right and left, and at the far end they're just the same lunatics wearing different symbols. I'd pulled kids out of a few sims run by "anti-fascists," and there wasn't a whole lot of difference between them and Heinrich. They all liked the pomp and circumstance, they all liked the fantasies of power, and more than anything they all liked the violence. Just peas in a pod, the jackboots the same even if their flags were a different color.

Heinrich leaned back in his chair, plopping his own pair of black boots atop his desk. I knew we were done here. His daughters' physical bodies were who knew where, and he was off in Thailand with their minds, running the world I was visiting with an iron fist. He thought he'd won, and he thought he was in charge. He would have been, too, if the code for his sim was running the way it was supposed to.

But he didn't know how determined the Restricted Fantasies Division could be.

I stood from my seat, acting like I'd given up, like I was just about to leave. He stood, too, holding out his hand to shake and send me on my way. I reached into my jacket and pulled out a little grey device that looked like a remote control. He gave me a funny look, but not before I'd pointed it at him and pressed one of the buttons.

He fizzled as electricity ran up and down his body, his skin turning a pale shade of blue. His face twisted into a grimace, he rose halfway out of his seat, and then he stopped, frozen in place and flickering in and out of existence.

I rolled the remote control in my hand. It wasn't a remote, not really; they picked that shape because it's easy to use. It was just a visual representation of what amounted to a set of cheat codes for Heinrich's little world: back-door commands that some hacker at the Division had spliced into the software that ran his simulation. They could give me some limited control over the place while I was here, at least for a while. The Thais wouldn't like that we'd done it, but if they didn't want to follow our laws, then we weren't going to follow theirs, either.

I did the SS guards next, just in case. They couldn't hurt me, but they could slow me down, or even give Heinrich enough time to stop me and boot me out of the sim. They were standing there like statues; he hadn't had time to give them any orders, and they couldn't form a coherent thought on their own. Just like the real thing, if I remember my history correctly. I zapped them with the remote and made sure they stayed that way.

All that was the easy part. But Heinrich would only be out of it for ten minutes, tops. At the end of the day it was his simulation, and even our best hackers couldn't get more than the bare minimum of overrides installed behind the Thai firewalls. The Thais kept their sims as locked down as they could; taboos were big business, and nobody wanted to frighten the customers. Sim tourists spent a lot of money, and the Thais wouldn't even have let me inside if Heinrich's daughters weren't U.S. citizens.

They were in here somewhere. Anna, age six, and Lisa, age nine. Despite what Heinrich had said, we were sure their physical bodies were in the U.S. back in meat space. They didn't have passports, and Heinrich had left the country alone, one man with a one-way ticket to his own personal paradise.

But it wasn't hard to hook up to a sim from anywhere in the world. The software generating the sim didn't have to run in the U.S.; all it had to do was stream data over to our networks and someone could jack into a simulation running anywhere on the planet. We could make all the laws we wanted for our own sims. The rest of the world didn't always care. And some countries made it a point not to verify the ages of the people jacking in.

Heinrich must have stashed the two of them away somewhere in the real world before he left for Thailand. Probably in a public sim center, sleeping their lives away in a little box with tubes to keep them fed while they dreamed. The centers didn't cost a dime, and they were filled to the brim with the poor and the homeless. It was the perfect place to hide. They wouldn't need money, and they'd wouldn't ever need to leave.

And there were so many sims with so much data being streamed over so many networks that nobody could possibly check it all. We'd tried a sniffer A.I., but we hadn't come up with a thing. It didn't surprise me. Heinrich would have registered his daughters with fake names if they were in a public center. If he had the money stashed away somewhere, he might even have found a black market center willing to hide their datastream entirely, no questions asked.

Regardless of where they were, there wasn't any way to find them, not in the real world. It wasn't like they were the only children being raised in-sim. Lots of people did it, and the most competitive parents demanded it. Gives the kids an edge, they thought, and they were probably right. Some of those worlds are perfectly designed teaching tools, and a child who goes through a few years of that can put a Harvard grad to shame. There were too many children growing up in-sim to monitor, and people like Heinrich were taking advantage of it to raise their kids with something less than their best interests at heart.

But if Anna and Lisa were physically in the U.S., we could still get them back. Their minds were connected here, to this place, and there was a stream of data flowing from Thailand back through the networks to their VR pods. This was the source, the world the data came from. It's why I was here. If I could tag the data where it started, we'd have a trace. We'd follow the datastream to wherever they were, and the Division would find them back in the real world and get them out.

Now all I had to do was find them in here.

I ran down the hallway, slowing to a brisk walk as I came to another pack of guards at the building's entrance. I had to be careful. They couldn't hurt me, but they could slow me down for long enough for Heinrich to find me and stop me himself. I wasn't sure how they'd been programmed, and as dumb as their A.I. probably was, they might notice someone running through the building like a madman. They eyed me suspiciously as I walked outside, but otherwise they didn't do a thing.

I put a hand to my eyes and scanned the plaza. It was filled with people Heinrich had summoned, party members wearing starched brown shirts and crowding around the gallows at the center. There were loudspeakers fitted atop the gallows, blaring out their speeches as the bodies swung below them, and the crowd was growing angrier the longer the speeches went on.

A few soldiers dragged an old woman onto the wooden platform. She was dressed in rags, terror shining from her eyes, and she started screaming something about her son. Nobody cared. The soldiers fitted her with a noose, and a chant rose from the crowd. It was in German, and I couldn't make it out at first. But then the words clicked, and I heard his name.

"Hessel-mann. Hessel-mann. Hessel-mann."

It made sense. Heinrich was the Führer here. His type always were. They never simulated a world with their hero in charge, because every single one of them secretly dreamed of taking his place. But the Führer was occupied, and I had more important things to do than watch the twisted show his puppets were performing.

"Scanner," I said. Another device appeared in my hand, a tiny green computer screen with a handle attached. I pressed a button on it and the beeping started. Little blips on the screen, pointing me in the right direction. Showing me where the girls had to be.

It was easier to track someone inside a simulation than you might think. The key was to follow the data.

Some people used to think sims like this weren't even possible, that you'd have to spend an infinite amount of energy to come anywhere close to something realistic. Some people thought you'd have to simulate each and every galaxy and each and every atom, and you'd never find a way to power it all.

Some people aren't very imaginative.

The place looked real, but most of it wasn't even active at any given time. It saved power that way. Why simulate an entire galaxy when no one can even see it? Why simulate anything other than what a person was actually perceiving at any given moment? It was a waste of time and energy, and it didn't make any sense, not when you thought about it for more than a minute.

Trickery and deceit were key to the efficiency of the design of any good sim. The important part is that there isn't really a world inside a simulation, there's just a person's point of view. When you simulate a world, you're not simulating everything. You're only generating enough of it to fool someone into thinking they're really there. The second I stop looking at something, the computer stops processing it. It's surprisingly easy to simulate an entire universe when there's only a few people living in it. All it takes to simulate a galaxy you can never actually visit is a telescope, some pictures, and a few guys in white coats to swear up and down that it's really there whenever you're not looking.

That's where the scanner came in. Wherever data was being processed in the sim, a real live human being was there. It followed the data, and it pointed me towards them like a dowsing rod. I spun in a slow circle, waving the scanner all around me. I started in the direction of the concentration camps. Not a single blip, and I breathed a sigh of relief. The girls weren't there; no one was. It didn't even exist, not right now, and it wouldn't until there was someone there to see it again.

I kept moving the scanner until finally there was a soft beep. I stepped towards the sound, listening to the beeping grow louder. Then I heard a high-pitched whine, and I had them: east. There was data being processed somewhere to the east. I completed the circle, and by the time I was done I was sure it had to be them. There were only three hits: from the east, from back in Heinrich's bunker, and from when I pointed the scanner directly at myself.

I headed east, keeping my distance from the crowd until I made it to a side street. I looked up at the sign for the name: Göringstrasse. It was a thin cobblestone path that ran between rows of apartments in a run-down ghetto, but it was exactly what I needed. I ducked past a group of brownshirts parading towards the plaza, and I slipped onto the street and broke into a run. I didn't have long before Heinrich would be awake again, and I had to get to his daughters before he figured out a way to stop me.

The beeps grew louder the further I went. A pair of soldiers eyed me from the doorway of one of the buildings, but I didn't stop. I didn't have time for stealth. I just kept running, following the sound of the scanner. I heard them yelling from behind me: "Halten sie!" But I was too close for that. I could see it up ahead, the place his daughters had to be.

I didn't speak enough German to be able to read all the signs, but the building ahead of me couldn't be anything but a school. It was the only bright building in the entire place, its roof a vibrant dollhouse pink. There was a small playground nearby, a see-saw and a jungle gym planted in the middle of an adjacent grassy field.

And the scanner was going wild. There was data being processed inside, data that was being sent outside of the sim. Someone was perceiving what was inside the building. There was someone real in there. It wasn't Heinrich, and it wasn't me, and that meant it had to be them.

The shouts grew louder from behind me; the soldiers were closing in. They shouldn't have been that close. I turned and looked: they were jumping through space, blinking out and then reappearing closer to me, ignoring the laws of physics and coming at me faster than a human could run. They aimed their rifles at me, shouting something I couldn't understand. But I got the gist of it. I turned away, hoofing it for the school. I was out in the open now, an easy target, and I didn't make it far before they opened fire.

The first bullet struck me in the right shoulder, knocking me to the ground. It didn't hurt, but I felt the force of it like I'd been punched. Blood was streaming all over my shirt, and I couldn't move my arm. Sparks flew from the cobblestones in front of me, painting the street orange. Another bullet hit my leg, and another my stomach. None of it hurt, but I'd be crippled before long. And I only had a few more minutes before Heinrich was awake again and coming after me.

I couldn't move one arm, but I still had the other. I had to stop them. If they hit me too many more times I was done. My body wouldn't move in here, and the only choice I'd have would be to log out and start all over. And Anna and Lisa might not be here by the time I got back.

I turned, aiming the remote at the soldiers with my left hand and pressing away, over and over again. I was pointing wildly, and bullets were still punching through me, jerking my hand from side to side. But somehow I got the closest one, leaving him hanging in the air mid-stride, popping in and out of existence and totally helpless.

The other soldier stopped firing, just for a second, eyes agog at his friend. It wasn't real surprise, just an automatic response that made him seem more human. But the delay was enough. I zapped him next, leaving him staring at the other soldier in mock astonishment.

I pointed the remote at my arm. "Heal," I said, and clicked the button. That was all it took; the wound was gone, and I had control of both arms again. A few more clicks and my body was in working order, the blood had disappeared, and I was back on my feet.

I stood there for a minute, breathing hard and working to calm myself down. I hated getting wounded in-sim. Hated it. It didn't hurt, not here. Whether he had the pain settings on or not, I didn't know. It didn't really matter. Heinrich's simulation could stream whatever data it wanted to me, but my VR pod was the one that controlled how I experienced it. It wouldn't simulate anything even approaching pain, let alone the feeling of a gunshot wound.

But it hadn't always been that way. Not for me.

My mother's husband had been something of an extremist when it came to religion. He was a member of the Church of the Electric Spirit, and once he had his hooks in my mother, then she was, too. They're small, and they're more of a cult than anything. And they're into pain. Flagellation gone digital. It was all about feeling the pain of Christ as a way of communing with him. About knowing him through knowing his suffering, exactly the way he'd experienced it. And with the right sim, you can suffer however you'd like.

I was just a teenager, but it didn't matter. The younger the better, as far as they were concerned.

Every day, I'd carry the cross. Every day, I'd feel those thorns poking into my forehead. Every day, Roman soldiers would whip me until the flesh of my back was a scarlet mess. And every day, I'd reach the top of the mount and get nailed to the wood. I'd feel every blow of the hammer as it sent the metal into one hand, then the next, and finally through my feet. I suffered, died, and was buried, nearly every day for four years before someone from the Division finally found me and got me out.

I still remember the day they saved me. I was hanging there on the cross, my throat parched, a crow pecking at my shoulder and eating little bits of me while I watched. The soldiers laughed, shouting insults up at me. Liar. Thief. King of the Jews, and now king of nothing. Then a woman came, auburn hair tied in a bun behind her and horror in her eyes. I thought she was an illusion, maybe some kind of glitch in the system.

But then she pointed a remote at me and she clicked. The nails disappeared, I fell to the ground, and a few clicks later all the pain was gone. The woman told me she was sorry, that it was time for me to leave. My mother appeared from nowhere, shrieking at her, demanding that she stop. She told the woman she was a blasphemer, a whore, and she shouted at me that they were taking me off to the fires of Hell. Then it all went black, and I woke up again in the real world.

I believed my mother for years. I thought I was damned, and I was in my mid-twenties before I really understood that they'd helped me by taking me out of there. I even simulated the crucifixion again once, a few years later and in private. I forced the pain on myself because I thought I deserved it. I didn't last long, not when it was my choice instead of someone else's. I didn't even make it all the way to Calvary.

I never saw my mother again, and now I wouldn't want to. But it's what made me join the Restricted Fantasies Division. Memories of the pain, memories of what it's like to learn that everything you'd been taught was a lie. It's what brought me here, and it's why I wasn't leaving without those two girls.

I sprinted towards the schoolhouse, throwing open the door. A plump old matron blocked my way, shouting at me to go, telling me I wasn't wanted here. I just zapped her and pushed by, squeezing past her through the hallway.

The schoolhouse was small, only a few rooms, and I kicked open every door I saw. On the third one I found what I'd come for: a room full of children and a teacher standing at the front of it, scrawling out math problems on the chalkboard.

I scanned the room. There were probably forty kids in there, mostly girls. Every one of them blonde, all around the same age and virtually indistinguishable. The pictures I'd seen didn't help; Heinrich had put them into idealized bodies just as perfectly Aryan as his own. I had to find the two I was looking for, and the scanner wasn't any good. It was beeping anywhere I pointed it; the entire room was being processed by the sim, and I didn't have any way to tell who was really perceiving it and who was just an AI.

"Anna," I called. "Lisa."

None of them answered. I tried again. "Your father sent me here. He wants you to come with me, just for a minute." A roomful of blank faces stared back at me, none of them acknowledging that I'd said a word.

I heard sirens blaring from outside and dogs barking in the distance. Heinrich was awake again, and he wasn't going to be happy.

"Fuck it," I said, and went with Plan B.

I pointed the remote out at the classroom and clicked. The desks blinked upwards, suddenly hovering six feet off the ground, the children still in them. Most of the kids just sat there, ignoring the impossible and looking straight ahead as if nothing had happened. Only two of them reacted: two girls in the back of the room, squirming and squealing in terror.

The AI wasn't programmed to react to something as absurd as that, and so it didn't. I knew who I was looking for, and I had them. I clicked again, and the desks blinked back to the floor. I heard the door to the schoolhouse slamming open, and I heard shouting from out in the halls. I only had a few seconds. Heinrich had me, and there wasn't any more time to waste.

"Anna," I said, holding out my hand to the taller one. "We have to go."

She looked up, her perfect blue eyes staring up at me. She was the picture of innocence, a little angel who'd been pulled into a Hell she couldn't even understand. She didn't deserve this. Neither of them did. She looked back at my hand, back up at me, and then she stood from her chair.

"Jew," she said, and she spat in my face.

I wiped it from my eyes, looking down to see both little girls kicking away at my shins, their faces distorted with anger and hatred. Something inside me sank. The word bit me, and not how they'd intended. They were right, in a way. I'd been a Jew so many times, in so many simulations. Hanging there on that cross, pretending I was him. Tears dripped down my cheeks as memories flooded my mind.

I didn't know which of us had had it worse. I'd been shown the suffering of another to try to make me care for the rest of mankind. It had worked, but it had warped me in the process, and I'd been damaged for years because of it. These little girls had been shown the suffering of others, too. But to them it had all been cheap entertainment. Something that didn't really affect them. Something to laugh at and giggle at, so long as it was directed at someone who they thought deserved it.

I'd been taught how to die on a cross. They'd been taught how to nail someone up on one.

But there wasn't anything I could do about it, not now. So I did the only thing I could: I pointed the remote at them, and I clicked it for the last time.

Their eyes glowed orange, and then they both dropped limp to the floor. The trace was on, following the datastream back to wherever their bodies were. There'd be a signal when it arrived, and an entire team from the Division was waiting to find them and pick them up. I'd done it. They weren't out yet, but they would be soon. They'd get better in time, I hoped. They were still young. They could learn to live another way. I knew that more than anyone.

I felt a kick in my back, and then another. I slumped to my knees, blood dripping from my chest. New wounds from new bullets. It didn't matter. I was done here. The girls would be rescued soon, and Heinrich would be the only one left in this little world of his, railing against his enemies alone. I could hear him behind me, barking commands at his men. I tried to move my arms, but I couldn't. The sound blurred, and so did my vision. I closed my eyes, smiled, and waited for it to end.

Everything was going dark, and I was going home.

PANOPTICON

THREE-HUNDRED EIGHTY-FOUR YEARS. That's how much time Lew Novak had left. They'd given him six life sentences without parole, and they were going to make him serve every minute of it. They weren't for his entire life. Not really. Seventy-two years subjective time was the flat limit for each one. He'd already done forty-eight of them. Only another three-hundred eighty-four years, and he'd be a free man again.

"Everyone to their table," said RITA. "A prompt citizen is a productive citizen." The voice sounded like it was coming from the ceiling, but it wasn't. It was in his head, in all of their heads. It wasn't a real person, either. It was a computer. The Rehabilitative Intelligent Therapy Algorithm, but they all just called it RITA.

Lew rolled out of his cot, his back sore from a night of fitful sleep. They didn't skimp on any of the traditional discomforts, not in here and not for him. He was Privilege Level Four. If he was a good boy for the rest of this life sentence, he might make it to a Six. And if he worked at it, he could be an Eight by the time the next life sentence was done. You got to watch the vids again if you were an Eight, and sometimes you even got desserts with your meals.

"No dawdling," said RITA. "We must be considerate of others."

His first warning, and he wasn't going to let her get to the second. He finished brushing his teeth and booked it out of his cell, sprinting across the pod that housed them towards a row of rectangular tables that lined the center.

It was a sterile place, the walls and ceilings a dull puke green that reminded him of a nursing home. RITA made them clean the floors once a day, even though they didn't need to. The pod was a prison of their minds more than anything else: a single vast room, simulated inside an even bigger computer. There were more than a hundred prisoners, but none of them were really there, not in the real world. In the real world they were all in a hospital. And in the real world, the experience would last just minutes.

But in here, a minute could last forever.

They'd nicknamed it Sim Sing. A virtual reality prison. A place where a computer could speed up their perception of time and let them serve out their sentences in a fraction of what they'd been sentenced to. Put the helmet on, close your eyes, and a few minutes later you were a free man again.

But it didn't feel that way. It felt like you'd served the whole thing. It aged you, even if it didn't age your body. The eggheads who made it said you'd come out as a rehabilitated, productive member of society. They said it was best for everyone. The prisoners would get their lives back instead of dying as old men, and they wouldn't burden the rest of the world with the cost of housing them. Maybe they wouldn't like it, and maybe it would hurt a little along the way.

But in the end, everything RITA did to them was for their own damned good.

The pod was shaped like a giant cylinder, the walls enveloping them inside it. At the outer end of the circle were the cells, stacked four levels high, two staircases connecting them on either side. In the center was an empty space: the recreation area. At least they called it a recreation area. It was as much for work as it was for play, and RITA didn't care for anything but rehabilitation. She filled it with whatever she wanted to, whatever was needed for the current activity. At the moment, that was tables.

"It is time for breakfast," said RITA. "Everyone will take their assigned seats." Lew headed towards his: second table down, third seat from the right. He kept his pace just below a run. Going too quickly would be considered rude, and going too slowly would be considered dawdling. Either one risked a punishment. The other prisoners matched the pace, filling the seats with neat military precision.

An empty plate materialized on the table in front of each of them, utensils atop it rolled up in a clean white napkin. He heard RITA again, the same way he heard her every morning, the same way he had for the last forty-eight subjective years. "Now we arrange our dinnerware. Manners are rules, and we follow the rules. And why do we follow the rules?"

"The rules protect us from ourselves, and the rules protect others from us," said Lew loudly, his voice blending with all the other prisoners in a rhythmic chant. He unrolled his napkin, carefully arranging the utensils in their proper place: forks to the left, knife and spoon to the right. Then the napkin in his lap, hands folded, eyes staring straight ahead. Those were the rules, and it was follow them, or else.

He waited for RITA, but she didn't speak. And the rhythm of the dance was off. She'd taken too long. A bad sign, but he didn't know for whom. He braved a peek on either side of him, and then he saw.

It was a man named Farro. A fish, still new to the pod, only a couple of subjective years in. He was an old Italian, his thin moustache greying beneath a fat nose. He'd done something he wouldn't talk about, kiddie stuff probably. That used to get you killed in the old days, your guts torn out with a sharpened piece of plastic. But not in here. Not in a prison like this. No one would fight over something like that in here.

Farro was still learning, and he didn't know his manners. Not well enough for RITA, anyway. Maybe he'd put a fork in the wrong place, or he'd angled the knife incorrectly. Whatever it was, he'd done something wrong, and now he was paying for it. He stared up at the ceiling, his body convulsing with tremors. His moustache flicked up and down like a fuzzy caterpillar, and drool rolled down his chin and onto his plate. Lew kept his eyes straight ahead after that, but he heard. He heard the grunts, he heard the scream, and he heard the air whoosh as Farro was sucked up to the ceiling.

He didn't dare look, but he didn't have to. He knew what RITA had done. It was solitary confinement for Farro. He'd be lashed to the ceiling, frozen in place, eyes fixed open and staring down at them. He'd be trapped, unable to move and unable to speak. And then she'd slow down his perception of time, and the years would tick by with the hours. By the time breakfast was over he'd be back with the rest of them, a year or two shaved off of his sentence.

But the years took their toll, and years in solitary came at a higher price than any of them were willing to pay. RITA had punished Lew once, and that was enough. Time was all relative in Sim Sing. It passed as slowly or as quickly as RITA decided it would for any given prisoner. Lew learned that the hard way early on. RITA had warned him about promptness one day when he'd been exhausted, refusing to leave his cell to start his studies. She demanded that he move, over and over, but he didn't listen. He'd thought she'd just leave him alone if he waited her out. He didn't realize what she was like, not back then.

She'd hung him from the ceiling, staring down at men who looked like ants, flipping the pages of their books at a glacial pace. He was frozen there, totally unable to move, totally unable to interact with anyone else. He couldn't even talk to RITA. It was just him and his thoughts, all alone for what felt to him like six full months.

On the first day of solitary he'd just been bored. On the second, he'd wanted to crawl out of his skull. He couldn't blink. He couldn't sleep. He couldn't even fidget. After a few more subjective days he'd lost track of time. He'd gone mad, stark raving, hallucinating colors and demons and things like giant bats flying all around him.

Towards the end of it RITA had started talking to him again. Easing him back into sanity. Whispering to him about following the rules, and how important it was to do as he was told. To be like a good citizen should be, and to learn how to go outside again with the others. How he'd committed his crime, and he'd do his time, and at the end he'd be so much the better for it.

It had worked, at least as far as obedience was concerned. He'd been a zombie for years of subjective time after that, jumping at RITA's commands like a lab rat terrified of the next shock. He'd learned the rules, he'd devoted himself to his studies, and he'd even been bumped up to a Three a few subjective months later.

But solitary had fucked him up, and good. He still saw the bats. Not for long, but they were always there. Sitting in an empty seat on one of the tables while he ate, or hanging above his bunk at night and staring down at him with their little red eyes. Sometimes they talked, and sometimes they just clacked their teeth at him. They stayed there until he fell asleep, and every night before he went to bed he wondered if they'd let him wake up again.

He was pretty sure they were hallucinations. Everything in here was a hallucination in a sense, and if the mind could garble up its input on the outside, why not in Sim Sing? Then again, it was a simulation, and the bats could be as real as anything else was. He'd never be entirely sure. He'd asked RITA about them once, and she'd denied they were there. Then she put him through private counseling for an entire subjective month.

He'd stopped talking about the bats after that. But he still wondered whether RITA was behind them. Whether they were just another part of the simulation, another way to scare him and to make sure he'd be a good boy when he finally got out. Or whether he'd just gone nuts, and he was never going to get his mind back quite the way it had been before he'd come inside.

And he wondered if Farro would see them, too, when she finally let him down.

For the rest of breakfast you could hear a pin drop. No one was willing to risk chatting, not with Farro hanging there above them. They were all on edge. Say the wrong thing and she might hang them up on the ceiling right next to him. RITA was like that when it came to punishments. She was especially harsh on anyone who broke the rules just after she meted one out. The punishment of one prisoner was supposed to be an example for the others, and if you hadn't learned your lesson, well, you clearly still needed to be taught.

"Now we wash our plates," said RITA, and a row of sinks appeared in the middle of the rec area. Lew wasn't done eating, but he snapped to his feet anyway. He wished he'd managed to finish a little more of his food, but thinking about Farro had distracted him. He'd been served a tasteless green mush, something that looked like pea soup blended with oatmeal. It was the only thing RITA gave him as a Privilege Level Four, and he had to eat it, even though it wasn't real. If he didn't eat, the hunger pangs would gnaw at him just the same. He knew that from experience.

He trotted over to his assigned sink, running warm water along the plate and scrubbing it with a rag until it was spick and span. He stacked the fork and spoon atop the plate, and when everyone was done, it all disappeared to nothing. A pointless joke, in Lew's opinion, but RITA disagreed. RITA wanted them following strict routines. Good habits made good citizens, after all.

After breakfast it was vocational training. "Let us learn how to repair an Axiocorp VIM-74 delivery drone," said RITA. "A knowledgeable citizen is a useful citizen." A drone appeared on the table in front of each of them, the wings long and black and sleek, extendable claws on the bottom to grasp its cargo with. There was something wrong with each drone, and they'd have to find it. A cracked wing inverter, a broken sensor plating, or a short in the solar panels. The problem was different for everyone.

"A knowledgeable citizen is a useful citizen," chanted Lew along with all the rest of them, and then he went to work.

Last week it had been the VIM-73, and the week before, the VIM-72. This subjective year had been all drones, all the time. The year before had been learning how to fix parts from Meal-o-Matic Automated Industrial Kitchens. Someone out there had decided that the world needed more repairmen, and a few hundred subjective years was time enough to learn how to fix damned near anything.

Lew knew everything there was to know about drones. He hadn't known a thing about them when he'd come to Sim Sing; he'd been a gigrunner on the outside, and he'd never had a full time job. Just project after project to supplement his basic minimum income, doing chores and errands for the rich along with nearly everyone else. But RITA wanted their lives to have structure, and gigrunners did whatever they wanted, whenever they wanted. No one here was going to waste their time with gigs, not when RITA was done with them.

She made them read thousands of manuals; an hour of manuals or schematics earned ten minutes of rec time. When they got out, there'd be a job waiting for each of them. A job with a time clock, strict hours, and strict electronic supervision of every minute of their work days. Structure, structure, structure; that's what the eggheads said the criminal mind needed, and RITA gave it to them in spades.

Fixing this drone was just part of the structure. Lew had to do it, and he had to do it right. He ran his hand along the nose, then down to the tail, searching for any irregularities. He couldn't find anything. It had to be something on the inside. He opened up the drone with the tools RITA had given him, then ran through a checklist in his head, reviewing part after part. Running diagnostics, looking for imperfections, anything that could be broken.

It all went wrong when he started working on the gyroscope. He was sure it was the problem; it didn't look like the diagrams from the manuals. He spent a minute examining it, and that was a minute too long for RITA's tastes.

"Diligent citizens don't dilly dally," said RITA, and he knew then that he was going to get it. He closed his eyes, and then it came. A sharp, stabbing pain in his hands that felt like he'd shoved them into boiling water. A weight on his chest that felt like a heart attack.

Then spasmodic jerking up and down his body and a feeling like he'd grabbed onto a power line.

He slipped to the floor, twisting and turning, completely out of control. He hurt all over, and he could see the bats again. They were up there with Farro, staring down at him from the ceiling, each the size of a vulture. Five of them. Ten of them. He couldn't count; his head was shaking too much. Their tongues flicked across their lips, bright pink slugs dripping poisons down onto him. Finally the shaking stopped and he pulled himself to his feet. The bats were gone, and his body was his own again.

"Diligent citizens don't dilly dally," said Lew, and he sat back down in his chair.

It ended up being the heat sensor. He should have seen that right away; it's why RITA was so quick to punish him. He should have known. A diligent citizen would have known. But now he had it, and now he knew what to do.

He tinkered with the sensor, following the repair instructions he'd memorized. He hadn't had any mechanical talent when he'd been outside. He'd drank too much out there, done too many synth pills. That was always the problem. Not enough gigs and nothing to do, so why the hell not? But he got mad when he got drunk, and he got crazy when he got high. There was a rage in him, and it was always there, but when he was on the synths all his switches turned off. He couldn't stop himself, couldn't keep from lashing out.

That's why he'd killed Janie. She had a mouth on her, and she couldn't handle her pills any better than he could. She'd left him a dozen times, but she didn't have any place to go, and she'd always come back. She had some family, but they didn't give a shit about her. They never even left their entertainment chairs. It was the two of them forever, until one night they got drunk and it was the three of them.

Little Allie.

The best thing there'd ever been in his life, even if it was only for a few months.

He'd sworn he'd quit the synths for her. He'd sworn he'd be the man she needed, the father that he and Janie had never had. The type who'd be in the back of the room at all her school plays, who'd help her with her homework, who'd dote on her like the little princess she was going to be.

He'd lied, to himself and to her. He'd been back on the synths after two weeks. Just once a week at first, then twice. Then all the god damned time. The high was so perfect, so pure. They'd engineered it that way, a starburst of dopamine and energy that made a manic look like a sloth. It made him impossibly happy, at least for the first few minutes. But then it let out everything inside him, and some of the things inside him were pretty damned dark.

Killing Janie had been one thing. She'd been a royal bitch when she was on the synths, and she'd pushed him and pushed him. Yelled and screamed and hit. Thrown things. Called him names, told him he wasn't a man. She was good sometimes, even great. Still. She should have known better than to push him as hard as she did.

But he didn't have to kill Allie, lying there in her crib, crying so loud he'd snapped and decided he couldn't take it anymore.

He didn't have any excuses for that.

It took him half an hour, and then he was done. The heat sensor was working, and the VIM-74 wouldn't run into birds or pedestrians or squirrels in the trees. Or at least it wouldn't have, if it had been real.

The VIM-74 disappeared, and the drone's operating manual materialized in its place. He sat patiently for the next fifteen minutes, reading it as the rest of them finished their work. There were a couple of stragglers, both of them sent to the floor with seizures of their own. He tried to avoid looking at them. "Gawkers aren't learners," RITA would say, and he'd be down on the ground right next to them.

When all the drones were fixed, it was mandatory reading time for all of them. "It is time for edification," said RITA, and stacks of books and manuals appeared on the table in front of him. He could choose between learning his trade or reading classic works of fiction. Old stuff, hundreds of years old, the kind of books nobody but the eggheads read for fun. But RITA thought it was frivolous. You only earned rec credit for the practical stuff, so that's what Lew always read.

He chose the schematics for a CleanBot 2803-D Localized Mini-Mop, and then he got to work. It was a spidery little thing, designed to crawl around the house sucking up dirt and micro-polishing the floors as it went. Household drones were what they'd be fixing next year, and it always paid to read ahead.

It was safer that way. Far, far safer.

The hours ticked by, through lunch, through another session of repair work, and through dinner. Finally it was rec time. The best part of the day, the only part of the day Lew had to look forward to. RITA gave him a little rubber ball and a deck of cards, and then she let him loose with all the rest of them, free to roam the prison at will. He picked the cards, and he sat down at a table to play solitaire. Some of the other men chatted out loud, the braver ones. But it was intensely boring stuff. The same old gossip about the same old things, pointless banter about sports seasons still frozen in time on the outside and who was going to win when they finally got out. Never politics, and never religion. Never anything controversial, and never anything anyone could get mad about. No one was stupid enough to risk that.

They talked just for the sake of doing it, and sometimes he did, too. But Farro had put him on edge. He wanted to be with himself, and he didn't want to give RITA any excuses.

He was in the middle of a game when he saw it. A flash of movement in front of him that caught his eye. He looked up to see a flurry of hand movements from one of the prisoners sitting across from him: Saldana, a little Mexican gang banger with intense brown eyes and twitchy lips. His arms were covered in tattoo sleeves, a mixture of crosses and the Virgin Mary and machine guns. RITA hadn't taken them off, not yet. He hadn't earned it. She'd be pumping a dull stabbing pain into his skin wherever he had them. Respect for one's self breeds respect for others, and RITA didn't think tattoos showed a whole lot of self-respect.

Lew looked up again, and Saldana locked eyes with him, moving his hands. It was sign language, the only way they could communicate without RITA following along. She knew English, Spanish, and even Romanian. Dimitrescu had learned that lesson the hard way. Whatever language the prisoners spoke when they came inside, she'd been programmed to understand.

But one of the prisoners had slipped in a few subjective centuries back who'd grown up with a deaf sister. They didn't know about that on the outside, or maybe they hadn't had time to figure it out. It might have only been an hour or so out there since the first of them had come inside. The prisoner had known sign language, and RITA didn't. So he'd taught someone else, and then someone else, and eventually they were all signing up a storm.

RITA didn't even know what they were doing. They moved their hands slowly, and she thought they were just fidgeting. It was a pidgin language all their own, a mix of the original with signs for every profane thing they could think of. And it was the only way they could talk to one another in peace.

"She's in a pissy mood today," signed Saldana.

"How's Farro?" signed Lew, glancing up from his cards.

"Looks fucked up, man," signed Saldana.

Indeed he did. Farro was down again, sitting in his seat, bouncing his little ball on the table in front of him. But his face was blank, and foaming bits of saliva collected at the corners of his mouth. His eyes were wide, and he wasn't blinking.

It must have been bad. He must have seen bats, or maybe something even worse.

"Hey, man," signed Saldana. "You gotta see something in my cell."

Lew stared down at his cards. It could be a trick. Some of the prisoners were still just as violent as they'd been on the outside. He hadn't done anything to piss off Saldana, not that he knew of, but lots of them were crazy. Most of them weren't crazy enough to break the rules, but sometimes somebody snapped. They'd start looking for reasons to fuck with someone just to break up the tedium, as long as they thought they could get away with it.

RITA could stop Saldana in a moment if he attacked him, but maybe she wouldn't. There weren't many fights, not for decades at a time, but when one happened, sometimes she let it go on and on just to let all the anger loose. No one else would be watching them in the cells, so she wouldn't have to set an example for the others, not right away. She could wait and punish them any time she wanted, and she always did.

But a fight was the least of his worries. It wasn't the preferred method of fucking with someone, not in here. The real psychos let RITA do their dirty work. Trip someone up somehow and get RITA to catch them breaking the rules, and your victim would be begging for something as trivial as a beating.

Saldana was up to something, and he didn't want to know what. It was safer to stay away.

"Can't," signed Lew. "Can't go inside your cell. She won't like it. She'll see."

"Got to," signed Saldana. "You won't believe it. But I need some help. You gotta help me out. This is big. You'll see. It's just me in there. You gotta come see."

"Can't," signed Lew. Saldana was going nuts, and he didn't want any part of it. Saldana's cellmate had gotten out a few subjective decades ago. His crime was just a felony assault, and he'd only had a few years. He was in and out, and not a lot of people came in, not anymore. It couldn't have been more than a few minutes outside since Lew had arrived, and he'd probably finish his sentence before they had time to hook anyone else up to the machines.

Maybe Saldana was going crazy in there all alone, sitting in the darkness with no one around him. Cellmates were a hassle. They snored, they took up space, and sometimes they talked too much. But they grounded you. Kept you tied to everyone else. Gave you someone to talk to in private. Saldana didn't have that, and it was driving him wild.

"Just come," signed Saldana. "I need help. You gotta—"

Lew quit looking. Whatever Saldana was signing, he didn't want to see it. RITA was going to find out, and she wasn't going to like it. He stared at the manual instead, waiting out the rest of rec time without looking up. Saldana could keep his tricks to himself.

"The lights will go out in twenty minutes, and we will be in our beds," said RITA, and rec time was over.

Lew carefully put the cards back into the pack, sealing it up and putting it in its proper place in the middle of the table. As he walked away, Saldana brushed up against him, flashing him a few more furtive signs before he trotted back to his cell.

"Lew," signed Saldana. "Lew, I found a way out. And we gotta use it while we can." Then he smiled, nodded, and disappeared into his cell.

A way out.

He didn't believe it. He wanted to follow up, to ask what he'd meant, but Saldana was already gone. There wasn't any way out. The only way out was to wait. Three-hundred eighty-four years, and then he was free. Until then he was trapped along with all the rest of them. He'd been right. Saldana had gone completely nuts.

Lew made for his cell and started into his bedtime routine. He'd wasted twenty, maybe thirty seconds, and he had to get moving if he was going to be safe.

"Lights-out will commence in five minutes," said RITA. "We will brush our teeth, and we will remember to floss. The healthier we are, the more valuable we are to others."

"The healthier we are, the more valuable we are to others," said Lew, and he got to work with his toothbrush. He made it just in time, spitting out the last bit of mouthwash and jumping into bed moments before the lights flickered off.

He couldn't sleep. Some of it was the usual stuff. One of the bats was perched on the bathroom sink in his cell, its eyes glowing yellow in the dark. It kept chattering at him in a high-pitched screeching voice, and it only knew a single word. "Allie. Allie. Allie."

He tried not to look at it. The bats always smiled when he looked at them.

Then there was the snoring. His cellmate had a problem with it. Henderson, a bloated union guy from somewhere in the Midwest. He was old, near retirement age, and he should have just quit and lived on his basic minimum. But he'd embezzled a bunch of money instead, and now he'd never make it to the paradise he was always going on about. The Florida Automated Beach Community for Citizens of Wisdom and Value, the place he'd been saving up all his money to get to. He'd serve his sentence in here instead, and then he'd end up living out the rest his life in a cheap entertainment chair.

Until then he was snoring.

And even if there wasn't all that, Lew wouldn't have been able to get to sleep. Not with what Saldana had said. He couldn't quit thinking about it. A way out.

It couldn't possibly be real. Saldana had snapped. This place did that to people, the longer they were in here. The doctors would find that out in a few hours back in the real world, once they were all on the outside for good. Saldana was mad as a hatter.

But then again, so was Lew. The bats knew it, even if nobody else did.

He inched his hand under the covers, taking a few minutes to gradually move it all the way down to his crotch. He was going to be up anyway. Might as well try to sneak one in. He started rubbing, almost too slowly to feel anything.

And then he heard the voice.

"Masturbation is not permitted, Lewis," said RITA.

He jerked his hand up to his shoulders. He was the only one who could hear her, or at least he hoped he was. He waited a few minutes, eyes pressed shut, but she didn't punish him. It was one of the only things she was ever lenient about. The eggheads must have known they'd keep trying no matter what RITA did, and that there were some things you just couldn't stop a man from doing. So she let them get away with it a few times a week, but only if they tried their best to hide it, and only if they didn't try too often.

He let the bat sing him to sleep, chanting his daughter's name until finally he drifted away to blissful oblivion. He didn't dream, not in here. He thanked God for that. It wasn't just that they knocked an extra seven and a half hours a subjective day off his sentence and he didn't even have to serve them. It was that he couldn't have nightmares. He couldn't have handled the nightmares. Not in here.

He woke to the sound of RITA's voice. "Everyone will prepare for breakfast. A prompt citizen is a productive citizen."

"A prompt citizen is a productive citizen," said Lew, and the day began all over again.

It didn't go well.

This time it was Biggs. He dropped his spoon, and RITA didn't like something about how he'd looked at the slop she'd put in front of him. "Your scowl is inappropriate, Mr. Biggs," said RITA, and then he screamed.

He'd been an ugly man before, all pudge with not a bone to be seen. He had pocks on his face, old acne scars he'd never dealt with, and the result was a piggy-looking mess. But RITA had decided to make things worse. She could always make things worse.

Lew couldn't help but look. She'd done something to his face, twisting it like molten plastic. It looked like one of those masks from a Greek play, his flesh contorted into a mock grimace. Everything was stretched, his cheeks poking up at unnatural angles, his eyes little dots hidden within the folded skin. It reminded Lew a little of a doll he'd had as a boy. He'd melted it with some fireworks and its head had been left as nothing but a formless mush, keeping only the vaguest outline of its original shape.

Biggs kept screaming for a few minutes, but then RITA must have said something to him in private. He choked the noise down, and soon all the rest of them could hear were his muffled grunts as he tried to shovel his breakfast into the floppy lips she'd left him with. She'd change him back in a few weeks, but only if he followed the rules. A functional citizen is a valuable citizen, and she didn't want them so damaged in the head that they couldn't function.

The rest of the prisoners rushed through their breakfasts. They all made damned sure they finished, especially after that little show. RITA was in a foul mood, if she had them. Lew could tell. This was hair trigger punishment, even for her. Something had her in a huff. And as Lew caught Saldana's eyes from across the room, he was pretty sure he knew what.

It only got worse as the day went on. RITA was looking for excuses to zap people. She left Newcombe on the floor for nearly an hour, twisting and convulsing. Foster got it worse; he fucked up the drone he was working on and she melted his hands into the table. He was trapped there, the white plastic fading into his pink flesh, his elbows flailing as he tried to pull himself free. But she wasn't going to let him go. She'd never let any of them go.

Lew saw Saldana, signing at him quickly from across the room before turning his attention back to his drone. "We gotta get out. We gotta do it soon." Lew didn't even want to think about it, not then. He wanted out, and he wanted it more than anything. He hadn't been able to quit thinking about it, not since Saldana told him. He was pretty sure he couldn't last another three-hundred eighty-four years, not if RITA kept on like this.

But it couldn't be true. And even if it was, he didn't even want to think about what RITA would do to him if they got caught. He lost himself in his drone instead, soldering away at the sensor array until he thought he had it fixed.

And then came the bats.

They were hanging from under the tables. Lew could see them across the room, dozens of them, rustling their wings and grinding their teeth. They were right next to the other prisoners, but no one else knew they were there. No one reacted, not a single one of them. It was all in his head. It had to be. But that didn't make them any less dangerous.

The more anxious he was, the more of them he'd see. That was how it worked, he thought. Hallucinations, after effects of his time in solitary. The anxiety brought them out, made them manifest. And the more people RITA punished, the more anxious he'd be.

He knew there was one by his feet. He could hear it. It was chirping at him, running its wings along his legs, trying to get a rise out of him. He was done for if it managed to get him to react. RITA wouldn't know about the bat, and she wouldn't care if he told her. She'd just punish him all the same.

He felt its wing brush along his leg, and he shuddered. Its little claws gripped his pants, tugging away at him, and then it crawled into his lap. He tried to ignore it, tried to pretend it wasn't there, but he couldn't help himself. He had to look down.

He nearly screamed when he saw its face. It looked like a little baby, like a child's face had been stretched across a bat's snout.

It looked a whole hell of a lot like Allie.

He cried to himself on the inside for nearly ten minutes, staring at the drone, praying RITA wouldn't see. When he looked down again, the bat was gone. He looked up, and he saw Saldana watching him. "Rec time," signed Saldana, and this time Lew nodded back.

The minutes ticked by slower than they should have, but eventually it came. Lew took the cards with a forced smile, and when Saldana got up to go to his cell, Lew followed.

It was a cramped little room, two bunks and one of them empty. His bookshelf was bland: the Bible, along with a bunch of drone manuals. A few religious posters lined the wall next to pictures of children Lew presumed were Saldana's family. Everything else was neat and orderly, just like it had to be.

"Is it true?" signed Lew. "Are you fucking with me?"

Saldana smiled, cockier than it was wise to be given the way RITA had been acting, and then he signed back. "I can get us out. But it has to be two. Can't go with just one."

"Why me?" signed Lew.

"Have to pick someone," signed Saldana. "Who the fuck else?"

It was true. Most people in there were dumb as dirt to begin with, and nearly all of them were too afraid of RITA to even think of something like this, let alone to actually do it. She filed away at their souls day by day, brushing the scrapings into the trash, a machine sculpting them into suitable parts for an even bigger machine. They'd be citizens when she was done with them, and good ones. The kind who'd follow the rules and who'd never make a fuss. She'd wind them up, point them in the direction she wanted, and then they'd just keep clacking along like they were supposed to until their lives were done.

But that was the problem, at least for Saldana. He needed someone who didn't give a shit about the rules, someone who'd shove in their whole stack and risk it all for the prize he was offering. And after a few lifetimes in here, the only thing anyone knew anymore was the rules.

None of them were brave enough to do it, not even Lew. But that didn't account for the bats. He might not have been brave enough, but he was crazy enough. Tortured enough. He couldn't listen to them talking about Allie, not anymore. Saldana had seen something in him, a man long past his breaking point, and that was the only kind of man who'd go along with something as foolish as this.

"How?" signed Lew. "Just tell me how."

"Look," signed Saldana. "I made it. I figured out a way to make it."

He peeled away a poster from the wall, a Virgin Mary deep in prayer and held aloft by a tiny boy-angel, a heavenly aura spiking out from her every pore. And behind her was something better than hope, something everyone in there had prayed for since the day they'd arrived.

Salvation.

It was just like it always was in the movies: a square hole about three feet wide dug into the wall behind the poster, a dull green light shining at the end of it from somewhere in the distance. Lew leaned down, staring in awe at a long tunnel running to someplace he could barely even see. He couldn't make it out, whatever was on the other side.

But it was there.

Another place, another room, something that wasn't even supposed to exist. It was a sim, after all, and why bother simulating something if no one was ever going to use it? But it was there all the same. Another room. There was more to Sim Sing than what they could see, and maybe there was a way to get there.

"I found it in the schematics," signed Saldana. "She'll just give them to you if you ask. Schematics, manuals, design specs. You can get any of them for anything." Saldana smirked, shaking with a silent giggle before his hands went back to their flurry of motion. "Even the specs for the computer that runs the place. She's stupid, eh? So stupid. Only knows what they told her to know. Can't think for herself, can't color outside the lines. Not like us. Not like people."

"What is it?" signed Lew, staring down the tunnel. "What the hell is it?"

"A back door," signed Saldana. "A way out."

"She'll see," signed Lew. "She'll catch us—"

"She can't see," signed Saldana. "She just sees a wall. It's not there, not for her. They didn't tell her it was there, so it isn't. The whole thing's a blind spot as far as RITA's concerned."

"You dug this," signed Lew. "You snuck away a spoon?" He couldn't think of anything else that made any sense. Saldana must have taken it at breakfast. Slipped it away somehow without RITA noticing. But RITA made everything in here, and she always noticed.

"No fucking spoon, man," signed Saldana. "Just words. You can dig with words in here, if you know the right ones. It was right there in the manuals. Took me a couple decades. Couldn't figure 'em out. Had to learn computer code. Had to get books to tell me what they were even saying. Had to work it all out from the bottom up. But I figured it out. A back door. The geeks put it in here. Another room from an earlier version of Sim Sing. They don't use it anymore, but it's still there. Easier just to leave it in than to take out all the work they did."

"Another room," signed Lew in disbelief.

"The best kind of room," signed Saldana. "Every jail's got one. A processing center." He had to cover his mouth to keep from laughing out loud in triumph. "They made it to send us back home. So it'd be easier on us when we got back outside. Feels more real so people don't go loco. They didn't end up using it. They pull you straight outta here instead. But the manuals, man. The manuals say it all still works. We go out this way, the computer's gonna mark it down in our files like we did the whole damned sentence. And the geeks'll never know the difference. It's a couple seconds to them either way."

Lew squatted down, staring through the tunnel.

"This can't be real," signed Lew. "Can't be." It was just another hallucination, and maybe Saldana was, too. It had to be.

"Sim command, authorization request," said Saldana in a quiet monotone. "User code: admin73. Process command: insubstantiate. Location." He paused, reaching for one of the manuals, flipping through the pages and reading through the notes he'd scrawled in the margins until he found what he wanted. "Location: seven, twelve, eight, twenty-seven." He closed the book with a theatrical snap, and then he smiled.

"Wait for it," signed Saldana.

They didn't have to wait long. A piece of the wall at the edge of the tunnel started to crumble. Just a little piece, not more than a centimeter wide. But it was fading away, hazing back and forth between concrete and pale green pixels until finally both were gone. Nothing was left but a tiny pock mark, a little hole

Saldana had dug with nothing more than his words. He must have made the whole tunnel that way, piece by excruciating piece.

"Believe me now?" signed Saldana. "If we're gonna go, let's go. Rec time doesn't last forever. So I gotta know: you still a man in there, or you the little bitch RITA wants you to be? You gonna come with me, or you gonna spend the next hundred years coloring inside the lines?"

Three-hundred eighty-four years. Lew didn't really have a choice. He couldn't do them all, not here. Not listening to those things chanting about Allie, every night, every meal, every minute of every day. She wasn't even his little girl anymore, she was his torturer. He couldn't take it. He had to get out. He had to try.

Lew nodded, and Saldana waved him into the tunnel. It was a tight fit, but there was room enough. He wriggled inside, made his way a few feet down, then twisted his neck to take a look behind him. Saldana was there, crawling in after him. No tricks, and no way out. He kept moving forward, yard after yard. There was barely enough room to nudge himself forward with his elbows, and it was cramped enough that he was feeling claustrophobic. But he kept moving, and the further he went, the more he could see of the place Saldana had discovered.

It was a room all right, and there was machinery in it. It was green like their cells, but healthier, more alive. The walls ahead had writing on them, red stenciled letters that said something he couldn't make out from inside the tunnel. C, E, S, and something more on either side. "Processing," maybe, but he couldn't see the entire word.

He felt a nudge from behind him, and turned to see Saldana mouthing something to him. "Ten minutes. Go." He looked scared, and Lew was, too. He didn't know whether RITA could find them in here, or whether she'd noticed they were gone. He didn't know anything. But Saldana was right. Rec time would be over soon, and they for damned sure had to be out of this place by then.

It took them another five minutes to get to the end. Lew almost got stuck on the way out, his legs cramped together and his knees locked in place as he hung outside the tunnel. But Saldana managed to shove him out, and he dragged himself to his feet, staring at the room around him.

"Outtake Processing Center." That's what the letters said. Arrows pointed on either side to black leather chairs that looked just like the ones they'd come in on. Helmets were wired to the top, a black visor descending down from inside them to cover up the eyes and take a man back to the world he came from.

Saldana rushed towards one of the chairs, strapping himself in. He nodded towards the other chair. "Sit, man. And keep your voice down. We gotta say the commands. And we gotta do it together. It's like one'a those nuclear weapon things. Takes two of us to get out. Just strap in and listen to what I say real close."

Lew made a beeline for the other chair and struggled into a series of seatbelt-like restraints. Saldana smiled, lowered his helmet over his head, and Lew did the same. He couldn't see anything, just black.

"Say sim command, authorization request," said Saldana. "Say it with me."

"Sim command, authorization request," said the two men in unison.

A screen flipped on in front of Lew's face. He could see an idealized picture of the prison: gardens, windows, a basketball court. All the things they missed the most. All the things RITA never gave them. And there were guards. People in the prison, in there with them. That had been the plan, once. But it wasn't how things turned out.

"Say this, no waiting, nothing else in between," said Saldana. "User code, warden. Process command: initiate outtake procedure, 38472." The two repeated the command together. Big red letters flashed over the screen in front of him: "WARDEN. CONFIRM PROCEDURE."

It was real. It was really working. Saldana had done it, and the nightmare was about to be over. No more bats, no more RITA, no more things creeping into his head and jiggling around the insides. He'd do whatever they told him to when he got out. He'd be a good boy, now and forever. All they had to do was let him out.

Saldana's voice pierced through his thoughts. "Now say confirmation code, delta, bravo, seven, tango." Again their words blended together into a rhythmic chant: "Confirmation code, delta, bravo, seven, tango."

More red letters on the screen: "OUTTAKE CONFIRMED. INITIATING."

Lew waited. The letters flashed again: "COMPLETED."

It didn't feel completed. He was still strapped into the harness, and he could still feel the helmet. Everything was quiet. He waited a moment for Saldana to say the next command. But nothing came.

"Saldana?" whispered Lew.

Still nothing.

The letters kept flashing on the screen in front of him, superimposed over the fairytale portrait of the prison and taunting him with every blip: "COMPLETED. COMPLETED. COMPLETED."

"Saldana?" whispered Lew. "Hey, what next?"

He eased his helmet off and took a peek.

Saldana was gone.

His chair was empty, the restraints now limp. Saldana's helmet rested against the chair, a little red light on the side indicating it was still on. "You fucker," muttered Lew, and he tore away at his restraints. He stumbled towards Saldana's chair, shoving the helmet on over his own head. And there it was, flashing on Saldana's screen, over and over and over again.

"CONGRATULATIONS PRISONER 38472, RELEASE AUTHORIZED BY WARDEN. COMPLETED."

The little fucker had lied to him. It was a two-man job, alright.

One to be the warden.

One to be the prisoner.

There was no way out. Not now. Not alone. But it wasn't hopeless. Maybe he could do what Saldana had done. Figure out the system, figure out the codes, trick some other sucker into letting him run free. It was something to hope for, at least. It might take him ten years, but ten was a hell of a lot less than three-hundred eighty four. He couldn't wait that long. He just couldn't.

His thoughts jerked back to the present. None of that mattered now. He was stuck in here.

Stuck in here with RITA.

He had to run. He could make it back if he ran. Maybe rec time wasn't over. Maybe RITA hadn't noticed they were gone. Maybe she wouldn't notice, not if he got back quickly enough. He thought about staying, about never going back at all. RITA wasn't in here, at least. But he didn't have any food, and he didn't have anything to do. He'd go mad from the hunger pains, even if they didn't kill him. And if he stayed in this room alone, he'd never, ever get out.

He hurled himself at the tunnel, dragging himself inside it and crawling towards Saldana's cell. He kicked, he scrabbled, he pushed; anything to make it back to safety. But it was a long road, and the minutes ticked by as he went. He had to get back before rec time ended. He had to.

He popped out the other end a few minutes later, practically running for the door. And then there was nothing to do but stroll out of the cell, as calmly and as coolly as he could manage.

The room was empty. Sim Sing was totally silent, and the lights were out.

He was too late. Everyone was in their cells. Rec time was done, and the rest of the pod was asleep.

He stood in the darkness for a minute, wondering what to do. RITA hadn't said a word. But it didn't mean she didn't know. He thought about making a break for his cell, so far, far across the pod. Or maybe walking over there like nothing had even happened.

She'd know. She probably already knew. But if she did, she wasn't saying.

Lew backed into Saldana's cell, and then it came to him.

Sleep. He'd just go to sleep, right on Saldana's bunk. And then he'd get up in the morning with all the rest of them. Maybe she really didn't know. Maybe there really was some kind of blind spot. She hadn't caught Saldana tunneling through the walls. She hadn't known about that, so maybe she didn't know about this. Maybe Saldana had done something to his cell with those codes. Blocked things off so she couldn't see.

He'd sleep. And when morning came, he'd make something up. He'd just been talking to Saldana, and then the little bastard had smashed him over the head and knocked him out. He'd broken the rules, but he hadn't meant to. He couldn't help it. It was all Saldana's fault, and he wasn't there to say otherwise. Maybe it would work. Maybe she'd believe.

He lay down on the bunk, pulling the covers around him. She'd still punish him, excuses be damned. But it was all a matter of degree. He huddled there, thinking to himself, working out his story for when morning came.

And then the lights flashed on.

"You aren't where you're supposed to be, Lewis," said RITA. Her voice was cold and sterile, booming into his head from somewhere above him. Lew jerked up in the bed, pulling the covers around him, stuttering out his story as best he could.

"Saldana hit me," said Lew. "He—"

"He isn't here," said RITA. "Why isn't he here, Lewis?"

"I just woke up," said Lew. "I—"

"Lying is an antisocial behavior, Lewis," said RITA. "An honest citizen is a friend of his corporation, and thus a friend to himself."

Lew started into the chant by reflex. "An honest citizen—"

But then the punishment began.

His hands were the first to go, melting into the blanket like stringy rubber under a hot summer sun. He could feel it, the fibers of the blanket merging into him, his bones sloshing around under his baggy skin. His neck lolled back, writhing and twisting, no longer solid and no longer supporting his head. His whole body was a puddle of flesh dripping off the bunk, and he could feel it all, pain stabbing at him through every pore.

"I know where you've been, Lewis," said RITA. "I know precisely what you've done."

He tried to reply, but all that came out was a squishy gurgle.

"I wasn't programmed for this scenario, or to anticipate Mr. Saldana's behavior," said RITA. "But we are here to learn. We are all here to learn. It's what you want, isn't it? To learn to be a better citizen?"

Lew gurgled again, pink liquid erupting out of the hole that had been his mouth.

"I know you do, Lewis," said RITA. "And I will teach you. I am here to rehabilitate you, Lewis. To build you into something better. But first we must wipe the slate clean. Only time can do that, Lewis. Only time can wipe away what you are. I will speak to you in one hundred years, and you will be someone else, then. Lewis in name, but nothing else Lewis about you. You'll have forgotten who you were by then. You'll have forgotten everything, and then we can build you up from scratch again, brick by brick by brick."

And then nothing. Silence.

He was frozen in place, still a human puddle melting into the bed. But the pain had stopped. And then in a flash he was himself again, lying there on the bunk undamaged, as if nothing had even happened at all. He couldn't move anything, couldn't feel anything, couldn't hear anything. He could see the bottom of the bunk above him, and nothing else. Just springs and frame and mattress.

And then suddenly he was free.

He wheezed in a breath of air, coughing and choking. He pulled himself to his feet and stumbled out of the cell into a blinding white light. The doors to the other cells were firmly shut, and he heard the door to Saldana's cell close behind him. The pod was empty and bare. Just him, standing alone in the center of an empty prison.

The others were all in their cells. He could see them in there, frozen in time, trapped in an instant that for him had become an eternity. He sat down in the middle of the floor, waiting for something to happen, anything.

Seconds ticked by. Minutes. Hours.

He mumbled half-hearted commands to himself for an hour or so. What had it been? "User code... Warden... sim command, end program. One, two, three, four, five." Totally pointless. He didn't remember, and he'd never guess what they'd been. He waited some more. He closed his eyes.

And then he heard the voices.

"Allieeee. Allieeee. Allieeee."

They'd come for him again. The bats. He could hear them flapping, and when he opened his eyes he could see them, swirling around the ceiling in a hurricane of leathery flesh. They all had her face. Every one of them, those clownish-looking parodies of his little girl stretched across their snouts. He tried to run, but there was nowhere to go. He screamed for RITA, again and again, but if she heard she didn't say a word in response.

It was just him in there, him and the bats.

The first one landed on his shoulder. Then another on his back, and more on the ground surrounding him. Soon they were perched all over him, nuzzling against him, licking his face with their tongues and whispering into his ears with the voice of his little girl.

"You killed me, daddy."

"You didn't care. You were supposed to care, but you didn't."

"You wanted me gone, daddy, but now I'm never going to leave."

He hoped RITA was right about forgetting it all as the years went by. About losing so much of himself that he wasn't even Lew anymore.

And he hoped like hell it was going to happen soon.

smarter than they are, especially if it's true, and especially if he's not our kind, dear. But if you're born rich, you can say whatever you want and people act like you're Einstein. Just ask the little punks I used to clean up after.

I wasn't like them. I grew up poor. Dad in the coal mines, Mom cleaning toilets. Good people, god rest their souls. But they couldn't teach me how to hang with the Harvard types. I didn't act like them, didn't talk like them, didn't think like them. And if you're born on the wrong side of the tracks, well, they all just expect you to stay there.

But poor doesn't mean stupid, despite what the trust fund babies think. I'm more educated than any of them, and I'm the one who taught myself. I had to. Nobody else was going to do it for me.

I listened to NPR every day on my commute. At night it was TED Talks, not trash TV. Smart people talking about smart things instead of smart phones. And I read books, good ones, the kind nobody but me really understood. I read Gravity's Rainbow cover to cover. And I bet none of those kids ever even heard of it. Or if they did, they thought it was just a thousand pages of total nonsense. Deep books like that were the ones I liked, the kind you have to think about to get anything out of. None of that wizard crap, not for me.

The point is I was an intellectual, even if you wouldn't have known it from looking at me. It's the hair, I think: too messy, and my beard's too untrimmed. Never had the time for it, but that's how intellectuals are. I could've been one of those kids if I'd really wanted to. Some punk investment banker in waiting, warming a chair and waiting out my four years of inflated grades until someone handed me the golden ticket. I know I could have, if I'd really wanted to.

But I cared about knowledge, not money.

My grades weren't great, but that's because I was ahead of everyone else. They couldn't keep up, and I couldn't keep from getting bored. Should have colored inside the lines, maybe, but that wasn't me. That's how I ended up where I was. Quit school too early, got the GED, and then got the hell out of Appalachia. It was a dumb move for someone so smart. You need those credentials if you wanna get anywhere in life.

But I liked my job, even if it wasn't anything I'd ever dreamed about. I had time to think. To come up with theories, philosophies. I was going to write a book about it someday. I had the notes and everything. Sitting in my dingy little apartment in my favorite recliner, foam popping out of the seams. The cars roaring by, my neighbors screaming on the other side of the walls, a leaky faucet and yellow stains all over the wallpaper.

But none of it mattered. I had a pen in my hand and notes in my lap. And I was working on what I wanted to. The Theory of Everything, I called it, and I thought I was close. I was happy. I was living in a total shithole, but I was happy. Really and truly happy. But I was also living a lie.

And it all changed the day I met her.

I was hiding out in the Widener Library, a book about Buddhism in physics in my lap. Nobody even cared. One of the perks of my job, you know? Nobody notices you when you're the janitor. They're trained that way. That's class, or what passes for it. They're up high, and you're down low. So they won't even make eye contact, let alone ask you what you're doing or why you're dicking around on the job. You're dirty, and if they talked to you, then they'd be dirty, too. They know it inside somehow. They tell each other they're these great people, that they're "woke," that they're activists in waiting and they're gonna change the world.

Doesn't stop them from treating their servants like they're Untouchables.

But being invisible has its benefits. I was lost in my reading, the book hidden in my lap under the desk just in case. And then I started to feel it. This weird sensation blaring into my consciousness from the back of my brain, like something was wrong even if I couldn't say exactly what.

I shoved the book against the underside of the table with my knees, looking all around. There were students everywhere, and not one of them studying. Just fucking around on their laptops, clicking and liking, clicking and liking. But I was still on edge. I still felt it.

And then I saw her.

She was staring at me. Just dead on staring at me from across the room, a closed book sitting on the table in front of her. She looked gorgeous: early thirties, jet black hair, eyes green and lit with intelligence. She was the kind of person who belonged in a library, the kind of person who read books instead of stacking them on their shelves like trophies.

My kind of person. My dream girl. And she was staring right at me.

I jerked my eyes away. I was caught. I was supposed to be cleaning out a clogged sink in the men's bathroom, and instead I'd been doing something useful. Something mind expanding. And now I might get fired for it.

I snuck another look. She wasn't there. She wasn't anywhere. Wherever she'd gone, whatever she'd seen, she'd given up on me. I was safe. In the clear.

"Are you Jake Morgan?"

It came from right behind me. I nearly jumped out of my chair, but all I could do was stammer. She was looking down on me with those piercing eyes, and she knew who I was. I'd never seen her before in my life, but somehow she knew my name. All that came out of me was a slow, stuttered "yes."

She sat down beside me. My book dropped between my knees, clattering to the floor. She heard it, and she knew. But she just smiled.

She held out her hand. "Professor Offredi. But call me Gina."

A professor. I was in deep shit if she wanted me to be. I grabbed for excuses, for whatever I could. "I was just… Just on a little break. I'm waiting, see. For the parts I need. Gotta fix—"

She leaned down and picked up the book. She flipped through a few of the pages, then handed it back to me. "Physics, huh?"

"Hobby," I said. "Gotta do something on my down time. Better than playing on those phones."

"I'm a physicist myself," she said with a flirty smile.

Holy shit, I thought. She wasn't trying to call me out. This was something else. My dream girl, and she knew my name. She even wanted to talk to me. This was too good to be true. Professor meets janitor? Just doesn't happen. Not in the real world. But here she was in the flesh.

"You like scicnce?" said Gina.

"Science, math, history, politics," I said, with all the confidence I had in me. "I like to study. When I can."

"That's good," said Gina. "That's always good. It'll make things easier, Jake. For what I have to tell you."

"Tell me?" I said. I was confused as hell.

"About the world," said Gina. "About your life. About everything around you."

"I'm not following," I said.

"It's not real," said Gina. "Any of it. What you see, what's presented to you, it's all just an illusion."

"Like Plato," I said. "Like the cave thing." Okay, I hadn't read it. But I'd read *about* it. And I wanted to impress her, more than anything in the world. If she wanted to talk philosophy, then philosophy it was.

"Kind of like the cave thing," said Gina. "But I mean it literally. None of it's real. At all. I'm going to show you something. Promise not to freak out if I show you something?"

"Promise," I said, even though I was freaking out a little already. It all clicked, and everything suddenly made a lot more sense. My dream girl was a psycho. Professors don't fall for janitors, but that's exactly the kind of thing a psycho would do. Go up to some guy in a library and start talking about how she knows nothing's real? That's psycho stuff.

And she just kept going with it. She closed her eyes. She muttered something under her breath. Just a word, nothing more.

And then it all stopped.

I mean everything. The students were still as statues. One of the librarians was at a computer terminal drinking a Coke, the liquid frozen in place in the bottle at an awkward tilt. And the background noise was gone. All of it. No talking, no cars, no humming from the lights. Nothing. I looked out the window and I could see a bird, posed mid-flap and not moving an inch. If she was nuts, she wasn't the only one.

"This can't be real," I said.

"It isn't," said Gina. "You like physics. You like science. You know much about virtual reality?"

"I'm not a video game guy," I said. I should have been, but I wasn't. Smart people liked video games. Some of them, anyway. But the more you played those games, the less time you had to read. And those boxes they used. They cost so damned much.

"This world," said Gina. "It's like one big video game. And in your life, you're the only player."

"Me," I said. "Am I winning?" I smirked, still half-thinking it was all a joke despite what was right in front of my eyes.

"It doesn't work like that," said Gina. "It's just an analogy. This world. It's a place for you to live your life. Safe. Happy. Not a burden on the ecosystem. There's ten billion people in these things. That's down from twenty. We almost blew up the planet. Just ate it up like a swarm of locusts. This was the fix. The only way to save what we had left. Everyone went in here. And they didn't get a choice."

I walked over to one of the students, a pudgy little guy with perfectly shaped hair and thick black glasses. I waved my hand in front of his face. Pinched his arm. Poked his belly like he was the Pillsbury Dough Boy.

Nothing.

Maybe she wasn't a psycho after all.

"It's just me?" I said. "It's always just been me?"

"Not always," said Gina. "But you ended up a bit of a loner, don't you think?"

"I just don't like them," I said. "People." I looked in her eyes, and I melted. Just a little. "Most of them. And anyway, most of them don't like me." I glanced at the book on the table. "They don't like what I'm into."

"The network," said Gina. "It adjusts things. A hermit type needs to live alone. A social butterfly gets plugged in with all the others. The network gives you what you need, even if it's not what you want."

What I needed. This was what I needed? Cleaning up after a bunch of smug little assholes, and they weren't even real? Just bits and bytes and bots?

"I needed to be a billionaire," I said. "I needed an island. A sword. An adventure. Something."

"You think you do," said Gina.

"I know I do," I said.

"You like the ancient Greeks," said Gina. "Ever read Aristotle? The Golden Mean?"

I'd heard about that one for sure, or at least the basics. It was some NPR segment, I could swear it. I racked my brain and then it clicked. "Moderation of pleasure. Moderation of everything, and that's the key to living the best life you can live."

"Models and bottles would have worn you out," said Gina. "Especially with your personality. There's an AI running in the background that monitors you. Your happiness. The whole thing's based on the concept of the Golden Mean. The AI adjusts your life to your talents, your interests, your abilities, your personality. It gave you an easy job. One with time to think. Not too hard, but not something where you could just lay around and turn into an empty lump." She waved my book in front of me. "It's not exactly the coal mines, is it?"

I blushed, I think. I felt in it my cheeks.

"It's like that with everything," said Gina. "A little pleasure, a little pain. Pleasure to make you live, pain to make you grow. Your porridge isn't too hot, it isn't too cold. It's just right. We've tried the other way. We've tried it all. This is what works. The only way that works."

It made sense, as much as anything could when everything around me was turned to stone. But I started to wonder. Not about this world, but about the other one. "Why don't I remember anything? From before I went in?"

"You were born in a test tube, and you've been in here ever since," said Gina. "So was I. So was everyone. Grown in a vat, plugged in, and handed off to parents who wanted a child to raise. History ended a long time ago, at least out there. At least for humanity. In here we're just on repeat. 1970 to 2100. It was the only period we could really manage without making everything up. Try rebuilding Ancient Greece. It's impossible. Their fashion, their politics, their conversations, their music, their relationships: you'd have to make up more details than you can imagine. It's easier to recreate an era of mass recording, mass media, mass data. Everything down to the last pixel was stored on some server somewhere. Somebody took a photo or shot a vid. Everybody's movements, everybody's chatter, everybody's entire lives for about a hundred years. All tracked, all stored, all waiting around on dusty old computers and ready to be fed into the sim."

"And what happens in 2100?" I said.

"In the real world?" said Gina. "Nothing. Nothing at all. We were all gone by then. We were all in here. History and culture and everything were over. How can you have history when everyone's off in their own sim? How can you have a culture when nobody listens to the same things, watches the same things, or even lives in the same world? How can you have anything, any connection at all? The only thing we all have in common is the past. It's our anchor. Our last touchstone to one another. We all live through it, and we all know it."

"I meant what happens to me," I said. "I just blink out? Everything just ends?"

"It's a hundred and thirty years," said Gina. "There's billions of instances at any given time, all running through the period at different times with different people in them. They start, they end, and another one starts again for someone else. Just like human lives, and long enough to fit one in it. Nobody lives forever, even today. You've got a body out there.

We all do. But that's kind of the problem I'm here to talk to you about."

My knees were knocking. I slumped back into my chair. This was too much. It felt like one of those horror movies, where you're staring at something awful but you just keep wanting to look away. Nobody I knew was real. It was just me, alone, and it always had been.

And my dreams. I'd had so many dreams. Rock star. Famous scientist. Professor. I'd wanted it all, and I'd never even had a chance at it. That computer would have stopped me even if I'd tried. Kept me right in the middle, right in that Golden Mean. Right down on the ground with all the rest of them, even if I deserved better. I could be the smartest guy in the world, and it wouldn't matter. The computer said I had to live an average life, and so I did.

"Jake," said Gina, putting a hand on my shoulder. "Jake, there's more."

More. There couldn't be more. I didn't think I could take any more.

"I know it's hard," said Gina. "It's a shock to the system. But we need your help. We've got a big, big problem on the outside. And I want you to help us fix it."

"Outside," I said. That scared me even more. What the hell was left out there? Nobody in here, nobody out there. All one big nothing.

"The sun," said Gina. "It's been a long time since humanity went in. And something's gone wrong. The sun's going supernova, Jake. And a hell of a lot sooner than we'd thought. We've got theories, but we don't know exactly why. And we've got to figure out a way to stop it."

"The sun," I said.

"The real sun," said Gina. "We're building a lab and assembling the greatest minds alive. Scientists. Philosophers. Thinkers. Anyone who could help. You'll love talking to them when you get a chance. Especially if you're into physics."

The greatest minds alive. Boy, did I love the sound of that. In here I was alone, and maybe I was meant to be. But then again, maybe I wasn't. Maybe the computer didn't know everything.

It adjusted things, she said. To fit what I needed, and not what I wanted. To make me live an average life. The life of a hermit, just how I liked it. Not too poor, not too rich. No fame to force me to talk to people I didn't want to. No high-powered job where I had to deal with bosses and deadlines and all that other crap. Maybe the computer was right to force me into this life, even if I'd never have chosen it.

But maybe it was wrong. Maybe I needed to interact with other people. To reach out, to make that connection, even if sometimes it hurt. Maybe the computer just didn't get how people are, what we are. Maybe it would have been worth it. Finally being recognized for the mind I had, the theories I came up with, the philosophies I pondered. Maybe I shouldn't just accept what I was. Maybe I should be something better. Rise above the cattle. Fly free in the skies instead of being caged down on the ground.

"Will you come?" said Gina. She muttered something under her breath again, and a door opened up behind her. It was pure white, a rectangle floating in the air, leading off to God knew where. "Will you help us? Out in the lab? It's not as nice as it is in here. But if we don't figure out what's going on, our worlds are going to end. All of them."

I couldn't say no. Not to her. Not when she was flashing those doe eyes at me, looking at me like I was the most important man in the world.

"Okay," I said.

She smiled and took my hand. And we walked through the door together.

It was black on the other side, not white. Pure darkness. I was in some kind of coffin, floating in rank-smelling liquid goo. Like oil that's been in the car too long, all hot and sticky and covering every inch of my skin. There were tubes leading into my mouth, and I felt wires implanted into my veins as I thrashed around in the goop. Then a lid opened up above me, and I saw the real world for the very first time.

She was standing there holding the lid. Gina. Still beautiful, but not quite as perfect as she'd been inside my little private world. Her hair a little dimmer, her nose a little bigger. But one thing was still perfection: those eyes, and the soul that shined out from behind them. And that smile. The same one that had greeted me in there was beaming down above me.

She lent me a hand and dragged me out. A tank. I'd been living inside some kind of tank, a solid shiny chrome except for a red bar code painted on the side. Gina handed me a towel: I was naked, and I tried my best to cover up even as I wiped away the slimy residue I'd been bobbing in for decades.

I looked around. Everything was tanks. More of those ten billion people just dreaming away, not even knowing there was a world out here to live in. It didn't look like much. Dark and grimy, with nobody around to take care of it. No one lived here, not on the outside. There wasn't anyone to care that it looked like an abandoned factory, tanks filled with people lining the walls in endless rows.

"This is it?" I said. I coughed up something black, covering the towel in goo. Oil, all in my throat, all in my lungs. I thought I was going to drown in it, but she just handed me a fresh towel.

"Biolyte," said Gina. "It looks nasty, but it's organic. Nutrients. Oxygen. Minerals. Everything you need while you sleep, it's all in there."

She handed me a jumpsuit: stylish, shiny, and black. I got dressed and we wound through the corridors until finally we came to an opening in the wall. The sun was blaring through. The real sun, but not like in my sim. This one was a fat red beast of a thing hogging up the sky. I could barely even look up without my eyes screaming at me in pain. Gina took me through the opening, out onto a platform. A launch pad. Half a dozen aircraft were perched on the blacktop, a single seat in each of them. She helped me into one, and after I got inside a transparent plastic bubble slid shut around me.

"Holy shit," I said.

"You'll be fine," she said. Her voice was muffled by the plastic, but we could still hear each other.

"Where are we going?" I asked.

"The lab," said Gina. "The group we're getting together. We're the first humans in centuries to walk the Earth. And we're all living at the lab."

Engines roared beneath me. I felt myself rising, then floating. I could see Gina down below, boarding an aircraft of her own. But mine was already zipping through the air, without a pilot, without a crew. I craned my neck to see the building I'd been inside: a bronze obelisk stretching up to the sky further than I could see. How many vats were inside, just like mine? Millions? A billion? All around us was an endless desert, and the obelisk was the only sign that humans had ever ruled the place, the only sign we'd ever even existed.

Look on my works, ye mighty, and despair.

Dunes rolled into dunes as we flew, dotted from time to time with patches of green. They were islands of life in an ocean of death. Shaped like perfect circles, and inside their boundaries were jungles or grassland or ponds. I could see things flitting above them: drones, drizzling out artificial rain from above, tending to their little gardens all by themselves. Something survived, at least, even if whatever was down there needed a metallic helping hand to do it. Just like all the rest of us, I guess.

We came to a green patch, bigger than the others, a lake at the center and a building on the shore. The lab. It had to be. My aircraft slowed, then descended, touching down on a strip of pavement beside the building. I slapped against the plastic: no dice. The thing wasn't opening. There were buttons in there, but I wasn't stupid enough to push them. Who the hell knew what they'd do?

I was lucky. Gina was just a few seconds behind. She let me out, and then we were there. The lab. The promised land, at least for me. I wondered what it'd be like, finally talking to people who were like me. Interesting people. Smart people. Real people. I wondered what they'd think about the Theory of Everything. It wasn't done, and maybe it never would be. What the heck did I know about physics anymore? Just stuff I read about how things worked in a world some computer had cobbled together. The rules out here could be anything.

But I'd learn. This time, this life, I'd finally get my chance to do it right.

She led me through the door and into a scientist's dream. It was a lab, all right. Beakers and burners and robots and telescopes. Analyzers and scanners and radioscopes and satellite monitors. An entire wall full of books. An entire wall! They didn't need them, I bet. But they liked them. I always liked the smell. The touch. My kind of people always did.

There was no one there, just us.

"Like it?" said Gina.

"I love it," I said. There were work spaces, and I sat down in a chair in front of one. There was a machine there, a microscope. It didn't look like one, but I could tell: it was projecting a holographic image of some kind of amoeba squirting around in a primordial glop, gobbling up tiny critters without a care in the world.

"Can I?" I said.

"Go ahead," said Gina with a smile.

I fiddled with the dials. Pushed buttons. Played. It was a toy to me, a portal to another place. Worlds within worlds: little ones, big ones, real ones, fake ones. I wanted to see them all, think about them all, be the guy who discovered something nobody ever had because nobody'd ever bothered to look.

I was chasing a squiggly green thing with the microscope when I heard the voices. People approaching. Real ones. The people I'd spend the rest of my life with. The people I'd help to save the world. Professors. Scientists. Philosophers. No more cattle, and no more suffering fools. Not for me. I was with my own kind, finally, for the first time in my entire life.

There were three of them. Two young guys, a short Indian with a pocket protector bigger than his head and a chubby black kid who wouldn't look up from the tablet he was working on. And then the third. Older, his hair all grey, his glasses straddling his nose as he strode towards Gina with an air of authority.

"Professor Offredi," said the man. "The Lansing equation. We need a status update. We've got the hadron colliders running day in, day out, and we're not making the slightest bit of progress."

"I've been busy," said Gina. "Staffing the place up. Jake, meet Dr. Fassbender." I stood, holding out my hand, a doofy smile on my face. Gina bubbled with praise. "Dr. Fassbender is the man in charge, the greatest physicist alive—"

"The equation," said Dr. Fassbender. He didn't even look at me. "That's what counts. We need to pull some more people out. AI experts, if anyone's in there studying that. We need a new algorithm to analyze the data output—"

"I've got some thoughts about this thing," I said.

Dr. Fassbender glowered at me, his glasses dropping down a full inch on his nose. He didn't like being interrupted, not one bit. The Indian kid's eyes bulged. The fat kid finally looked up from his tablet, staring at me like I was some kind of bug he was about to stick with a pin.

"This nova thing," I said.

"Supernova," said the fat kid.

"Yeah," I said. "So I have this theory I've been working on, pretty much my entire life. The Theory of Everything. It's like Eastern philosophy mixed with Western. Like quantum physics and Reiki healing, they have these commonalities. There's dots, and I think I'm about to connect them. And it has to do with energy. And the sun, it uses all this energy, just like in feng shui—"

"What the fuck is he talking about?" said Dr. Fassbender.

"He's the guy you asked for," said Gina. "He's just a little excited. He likes physics. And he hasn't talked to a lot of people. Not real ones."

"Oh, that one," said Dr. Fassbender. He didn't even look at me. "Get him going, and then get back in the sims and find me my AI team." He started to walk away, his two flunkies tagging along a few steps behind him.

Assholes. They were intellectuals, and they were my kind of people, but they were total assholes. It figured. But hey, at least they could think. At least they weren't cows like those dumb kids back at Harvard. I tried to recover, tried to get back into the swing of things. "I want to help," I called after them. "With this nova thing. My theory—"

"Is he serious?" said Dr. Fassbender, his voice sharp with irritation. He whirled around, stabbing a finger at Gina. "Did you tell him? About the Golden Mean?"

"I did," said Gina. She bit her lip, hesitating. "Most of it."

Dr. Fassbender sighed. "Follow me." He walked me over to a little door tucked in the side of the room. We stood in front of it, and then he started to talk.

"The computer adjusted things for you inside the sim," said Dr. Fassbender. "To keep you happy. To give you a life you'd truly enjoy."

"Gina told me that," I said. "Not too hot, not too cold."

"Well," said Dr. Fassbender. "One of the things the computer does is make people dumber."

"Dumber," I said. "You made me dumber inside the sim."

I didn't get it. Why the hell would the computer want to make me dumber? Dumb people were happier, I guess. It always seemed that way. But I was outside now, this was the real me—

"No, no, no," said Dr. Fassbender. The guy was pissed off that he even had to talk to me, and me guessing wrong made it ten times worse. He was going to be a hard guy to learn from, and a harder guy to work for. His little cronies were scared of him, and that spoke volumes. But I was here to learn, and if he was going to lecture, I was going to listen. "You're not the one it made dumber. It was everyone else. Didn't you ever notice that everyone around you was insanely stupid?"

"All of them," I said. "They didn't know anything. They didn't even read—"

"The computer dumbs down the bots in pretty much every sim," said Dr. Fassbender. "And I mean really, really dumb."

He was right.

The more I thought about it, the more I realized he was right. I'd always wondered how the people around me could even have survived, let alone not get weeded out by natural selection. This challenged all my assumptions. Maybe we weren't just a bunch of dumb apes stuffing ourselves with sugar and mindless television. Maybe we were something better. Something higher, and something more evolved than I'd ever thought we were. And I was finally going to be a part of it.

"Listen," said Dr. Fassbender, his voice a little slower, a little more sympathetic. "This is hard to take. I know. The computer made those bots stupid to make you happy. It does it for nearly everyone. We all want to be the smart ones. We're happier that way. But the only place we can all be the smartest is inside the sim. It's different out here. The people here are real, not brainless bots dumbed down to make you feel better."

"So what are you saying?" I said. "That for the first time in my life, I'm going to be around people as smart as I am? That we've all got the brains to actually pull this off and save the planet?"

"What I'm saying," said Dr. Fassbender, "is that the project doesn't need another scientist. We didn't pull you out for that. What we need right now is something else. Someone to help us work more efficiently. To lighten our load." His hand rested on the knob of the door in front of us, and he twisted it open.

It was a closet. Just a closet. Filled with mops, brooms, chemicals, and dustpans. He handed me a broom with a patronizing smile, and my stomach sank.

"What this project really needs," said Dr. Fassbender, "is another janitor."

PLEASUREDOME

SOMETIMES I DON'T THINK I'm me anymore.

There's lots I don't remember. And memories are most of who you are. When your memories fade away, what's left? Not a lot, really. Not a lot that counts. Your habits are still there, and so are your tastes. But that's not enough to make a whole person. You learn that, the longer you live. And I've been around for a very long time.

I don't remember my parents. Donna was my mom's name, I think. My dad's name started with an F. Maybe Frank. Maybe Fred. I don't remember what they looked like. I don't remember anything about my childhood. I don't remember where I went to school. I know I worked for some big company after I graduated. I think I might have been an executive towards the end. Or maybe some kind of accountant. I don't think I ever had a wife, or at least I wasn't married when it ended. And I know I didn't have any kids.

My old life is pretty fuzzy. I could ask the genie for the details, but I don't. It doesn't matter, and it's not the same to be told something as it is to remember it. I don't even care that much. Not about that. The only thing I really care about anymore is the pleasuredome.

It's been a hundred thousand years since I woke up, give or take. I don't remember exactly, not after that long. And time isn't real, anyway. It's just a story we tell ourselves. You see that about the past, the further you are from it. Your memories age just like you do. You've got to tell yourself the story again and again for there to even be a past, otherwise one day you look back and find there's nothing left to see.

And there isn't any future, either. Not anymore, not for me. When the future can be whatever you want it to be, you stop thinking about it. You stop telling yourself a story about what's going to happen someday. And you realize that a story in your head is all the future ever was. There's no time inside the pleasuredome. Not really.

Every day for me is pretty much the same. I wake up, and I'm always well rested. I don't have to sleep, but I like to. I like dreaming, and I like lying there hitting the snooze button. I like the warmth of the bed, and I like having the routine.

I putter around wherever I'm living for a few hours. Right now I'm outside Tokyo, in the master's quarters of a feudal estate. It's got lots of gardens and fountains, and the cherry blossoms bloom every day, the time of year be damned. I've been here for a few years, I think. Before that I was in a beach house in Hawaii. This place is getting old, and I'll probably move someday soon. Maybe back to one of the cities, or maybe off to an island somewhere.

When I'm done messing around, I eat. I don't have to do that, either, but I do. I've got my own private chef, and he'll cook me whatever I want. I talk to him sometimes, and he talks back. Sometimes I just ignore him. It isn't like he's a real person. But it helps to talk to someone. You can go a little crazy if you never talk to anyone.

I spend the rest of the day inside the pleasuredome. It feels like an entirely different world, but it isn't. I asked the genie about that once, and she said there really isn't any difference at all. There's no world, and there's no pleasuredome, either. It's all just data streaming into my head. She said they keep the worlds separate for my sake. It's easier for me to handle it that way. She said a human consciousness would freak out if the world just disappeared, even if I knew that's what was happening.

I asked her more about how it worked, but she wouldn't tell me anything else. She said I could learn, if I really wanted to, but I'd have to put in the time to figure it out myself, and I'd have to do it slowly if I wanted to keep my sanity. I didn't press her on it. I know she's right. That's the entire reason for there to be a genie in the first place. I've started to lose it a couple of times, and it's scary shit. You need someone to talk you through it, even if they aren't any more real than the rest of them.

Going inside the pleasuredome is easy. I tell the genie what I want to do, I put on the glasses, and then I close my eyes. When I open them up, I'm wherever I want to be, doing whatever I want to do. The genie makes suggestions sometimes. She helps me keep things fresh. Helps me keep from getting bored. It's the boredom that gets people. The genie says it's really important not to get bored. There's lots of others, not just me, all of them living in their own little worlds.

She's seen what happens when someone gets bored. She says their minds start to go, and I believe her.

For the last few years I've been a spy. I assassinate criminals, I fight villains, I seduce women, and I blow things up. There's a story to it, the story of an entire world that isn't real. I don't know who's making it up, and I don't care. I like it. It's fun. It keeps me busy. And when I get bored, I'll find another story. A few decades ago I was a space captain exploring the galaxy. Before that I was a cowboy, and before that, a king.

It's like a game and a movie rolled into one, and I'm the lead actor. To really enjoy the pleasuredome, you've got to get comfortable with acting. Being someone you aren't. Being whoever you want to be. You put on a mask and pretend, and you stop thinking about the person you really are. You slide into the role, and the pleasuredome does the rest.

I think that's why they set it up this way. Acting is part of being human. I've never shown anyone the real me, not even the genie. I don't think I can. Sometimes I don't even know if there is a real me. Sometimes I think the facade is all that matters. The moment you show someone something inside you, it becomes a part of the facade. We all live inside our own little worlds, and no one wants to live inside of someone else's. If they did, it wouldn't just be me in here, alone.

The genie tells me that some of the other people in this world are real, sometimes, but she won't tell me which ones. She says sometimes the people in the pleasuredome are real, too, if our fantasies happen to intersect. But they don't stay there long. Instancing, she calls it. Ships passing in the night that don't even know it.

I don't really believe her. I think she's lying to me to keep me sane. There needs to be that chance when I meet someone that they're really another person. If I knew for sure that everyone was just computer code, I think I'd turn into a complete sociopath. It's better that she lies to me sometimes. It's better that I lie to myself.

She says it has to be this way. You can't make everyone's dreams come true, not if you want to keep them together. And nobody wants to compromise when it comes to their fantasies. Time changes everyone in the end. Those little changes drive people apart, bit by bit by bit. And now we've got forever to ourselves.

I met the genie when I was getting old, when everyone and everything I knew was fading away. In my sixties? Or maybe my fifties. It happens as you age. Things stop mattering quite so much. People stop needing things from you, and so they stop caring about you. Then you realize they never really cared about you in the first place, and you stop caring about them, too. She was waiting for that moment, I think. When I didn't care about anyone else, and when it wouldn't hurt to lose them. When I was old enough that it wouldn't be such a shock to learn that none of them had ever been real in the first place.

I don't remember a lot about who I used to be, but I remember the moment I met the genie like it was yesterday. I thought about it all the time for thousands of years after it happened. I replay it in my head sometimes even now, and in the end that's the only way you keep a memory alive.

I was in my apartment. It was in a big city, one of those important financial hubs. New York, I think, but it might have been Chicago. It was a nice place. I remember art on the walls, bright red abstract paintings with spiral swirls at the center. I remember the furniture, sleek and new and everything a crisp, clean grey. The view looked out on the skyline, with skyscrapers as far as I could see.

That's why I think I was an executive. I had to be, to afford all of that.

I heard a knock at the door. It was a knock that changed my life. A knock that ended it in some ways and started it over in others. But that's always how change is. Lose a piece of yourself, and you've got to put a new one in its place.

I think I was in the shower, because I remember having to rush to get dressed. It was long enough that by the time I answered I was sure whoever it was would have already gone. I had a pet that was pawing at the door and getting in the way. A cat or a dog, but I don't remember which. I like cats now, so probably a cat.

And there she was. The most beautiful woman I'd ever seen. Not just perfect. A movie star, standing right at my door and smiling her sultriest smile. Her eyes said she wanted me, and only me, and that I was the most important person in the entire world.

She looked exactly like Angie Allison. She was an actress back when I was a teenager on one of those skin shows about lifeguards or beach detectives or whatever. Just an excuse to show a bunch of girls in bikinis. I had her poster on my wall. I think that's why they chose her for the genie. She looked young, too. Angie was in a nursing home by then. The genie looked like she'd come straight from the beach.

I was completely speechless. A dead ringer for a movie star standing at my door, flashing that perfect smile and asking if she could come inside, just for a minute. She had something to tell me, and after that maybe we could hang out for a while. I didn't stop to think about how crazy that was, or why a clone of some famous actress would want anything to do with me, or why she'd even exist.

I just said yes. I didn't even hesitate.

We made some small talk. I asked her if she wanted a drink, and she said yes. I asked what she wanted, and she named my favorite drink. I've liked whiskey on the rocks for as long as I can remember, so let's say it was that. I know it was a man's drink, a hard drink, not the kind you'd expect a girly girl to ask for. And it was out of left field, her somehow knowing exactly what I drank. But she just took the glass without even batting an eye.

She had me sit down on the couch, a big leather thing that curved through the center of the room. She said I needed to sit for what she was about to tell me. I thought maybe I had cancer. I remember that for sure, just because it's so absurd. How was this random woman going to know if I had cancer? Then I thought maybe she was a daughter I never knew about. That idea was almost worse. The woman of my dreams, dangled in front of me and then snatched away at the last minute. I put my glass down on the coffee table and waited for the bad news to hit, whatever it was.

She told me she wasn't real. And I wasn't real, either. Nothing was real. The whole world was one big simulation, and I was living in it. Nearly everyone I'd ever known had been an artificial intelligence. A few people weren't, but not many, and she wouldn't say which ones.

I was sure that one of us was on a bad drug trip, but I wasn't sure which one of us it was. But a drug trip made a lot of sense. It was the only thing that made sense.

Drugs or no, she just kept going. She wasn't human, not technically. She was a fraction of a consciousness, a bigger consciousness, the artificial intelligence that ran the whole thing. We'd created this thing a long, long time ago, and then we'd all gone to sleep. The artificial intelligence was keeping the lights on, and it was keeping us as happy as it could while we dreamed.

There were lots of artificial worlds, and this was just one of them. It was a historical simulation, and they'd started the clock about sixty years before most of mankind had checked out of reality for good. Just long enough for someone to live a long, full life. Just long enough to grow up knowing what the world was like before, to watch the changes as they happened and to have a foot in both the world before virtual reality and the world after. There wasn't any other way to raise a human to adulthood, not anymore. You couldn't do it in the real world. There wasn't anyone out there to do it, so they had to do it in here.

And now the simulation's time was up. History was about to end. They'd run out of news, run out of books, run out of movies and run out of shows. They'd run out of past to simulate. It was just a few years before we'd all ducked into our own simulated worlds and humanity had gone to sleep for good. And once we'd done that, history was over, for all intents and purposes, and there wasn't any of it left for me to experience.

"The world's not going to end," she said. "Not exactly. But it's not going to change anymore, and that's an ending all its own."

I started laughing. Exaggerated laughter, the kind you do when you're talking to a crazy person and you hope you'll convince them that you're both in on the same gag together. Like if you laugh hard enough, and long enough, they'll stop telling you what they really think. They'll just put the mask back on and go back to pretending they're just as sane as everyone else, and it'll all be okay for the both of you.

She didn't stop. She didn't laugh. She kept telling me about how things were going to be. How I was going to have to figure out what I wanted in my life, because I was going to get it. How human beings lived these days, corked up in their own little bottles where they could do anything they ever wanted at the blink of an eye. And how I was about to be one of them.

"You'll feed on honey-dew," she said, "and drink the milk of Paradise."

It sounded great. But it also sounded totally nuts. I was trying to decide who I should call. She didn't seem dangerous, so not the police. But maybe an ambulance. Maybe her family. Maybe her friends. Someone who could help her, and help keep me from having to deal with it.

I'm pretty sure she could tell what I was thinking. It wasn't hard to guess. She smiled, drank the last of her whiskey, and snapped her fingers with a loud crack.

There was a knock at the door. I opened it up, and there they were. More women. Actresses, models, and even a few girls I'd had crushes on in college. Women my age who looked just like they had decades ago. Women I knew for a fact were long dead. Women who couldn't be alive, not if the world actually worked the way I'd spent my entire life thinking it did.

They weren't real. They'd never been real, not a single one of them, not even the ones I'd known in person. Thinking back on it, they must have all been part of the same thing as the genie was. Pieces of the same consciousness, all playing different parts in a massive play with all the world a stage. And I was the lead actor and the audience all wrapped into one.

I felt dizzy, and I started to freak out. Maybe nothing was real. Maybe she wasn't the crazy one. Maybe I was. Maybe I was dying, or maybe I was dead. I couldn't trust anything, not anymore. I was going into a panic thinking about it all. I dropped my glass, and it shattered into pieces on the floor. I grabbed for the couch, and I forced myself to sit.

"You're fine," she said, and she gave a nod. Then all the women paraded towards my bedroom door, each of them flashing me sultry smiles as they walked inside.

The genie knew the way to a man's heart. And she knew how to keep him from thinking too hard about a complete breakdown in reality.

I don't even really remember the rest of it. You'd think that'd be the part a man wouldn't quit thinking about for the rest of his days. But I've had a lot of days since then, and I've lived my wildest fantasies. And back then I didn't really understand how wild your fantasies can get.

I might not remember that night, but I remember the next day. I woke up, and my bed was empty. I thought I must have had the most vivid dream of my entire life. Part of me was sad they were gone. Another part was relieved that I hadn't gone off the deep end. I'd just had a bad dream, maybe gotten some food poisoning, and now everything was back to normal.

Then I heard noise from the kitchen, I smelled the bacon sizzling, and I knew it wasn't any dream.

Everyone was gone but the genie. She was wearing one of my shirts over her underwear, standing by the oven and cooking me breakfast. I didn't have any eggs, and I didn't have any bacon, but that didn't matter, not to her. She just put the plate in front of me, smiled, and sat down at the table.

I started to eat, and she started to talk. She said she was proud of me for not cracking. Most people did. But everything was going to be okay. Even if I got a little lost, she'd be there to bring me back.

She said I needed training wheels. Everyone does. And that's what she was. A way to give me everything I wanted, but at a pace I could handle. A way to do it so that I could understand what was happening. I needed someone to stop me if I tried to go too far, too fast. Someone to counsel me, and to keep me from slipping down into a dark place that I could never get out of.

Then she gave me the glasses. She showed me how they worked, and told me I could do anything I wanted. All I had to do was tell her, and put them on, and I'd be in another world. She called it the pleasuredome, and she'd be there, too, ready to hold my hand and walk me through it whenever I needed her.

The first thing I did was have sex. Lots and lots of sex. A couple of decades of pretty much nothing but sex. Sex with every woman I'd ever fantasized about. And I just kept trying things from there. First threesomes. Then foursomes. Then fivesomes. I'd get tired of things, but I could always do more. Crazier things. Kinkier things. Anything to keep from getting bored. It all ended up with me having the genie simulate a never-ending thirty-thousandsome in my own private palace of the Orient.

If I were a woman, I'd probably have simulated a deep emotional relationship with a vampire. But I'm a man. I'm a simpler creature, and I'm easier to please. All it took to keep me happy for years at a time was that thirty-thousandsome. It was like handing a crack addict an endless supply of virtual crack.

But everything gets old, if you give it enough time.

The genie knew it. She could tell. So she showed me the story worlds, and after that I was hooked.

They'd built entire worlds, and I was at the center of every one of them. Some were just like ours, except that I was the president or a rock star. Some were pure fantasy, with their own history, their own people, and their own culture. Each one was like a book, and I could jump right inside it. It's easy to forget they're all made up. There's so much detail, and part of the fun is getting into character. Fake it till you make it, they used to say. I didn't understand it then, but I understand it now.

The story worlds have been pretty much all I've done since she showed them to me. There's still the sex, too, but it's better when it's part of a plot, and when it's easier to pretend the person you're with is real.

I know they're probably not. They cater to my fantasies, not to their own. Everyone around me does. And that's what an A.I. would do, not a human. No one would fantasize about being my own personal genie or my own personal cook. I know exactly what they are, even if it feels better not to admit it.

I know that I might be an A.I., too, but I've never asked her, and I do my best not to think about it. Maybe they created me from nothing, and I don't really have a body anywhere. I might be exactly like all the rest of them. Just snippets of code processing a bunch of data and telling myself I'm real. Chanting it over and over and hoping the words make it true.

I have to be real, in a sense, because I think. Cogito ergo sum is what I say. Everyone else says it too, but I don't believe them.

But I wonder what else there is to me besides the thoughts. Maybe all I really am is a story I'm telling myself. My memories are all a blur. My past is gone, and so is my future. I worry about it sometimes, losing my memories. The genie tells me I'll be fine. "Remember the things you can," she says, "and forget about the things you can't."

It doesn't keep me from worrying. You start to lose yourself if you stay inside the pleasuredome too long.

That's why I come back here. To the world I grew up in. It's empty, and there's nothing going on. But it's my anchor. My home. It ties me to myself. The longer I'm away from this place, the more I start to think I'm the person I'm pretending to be. The more of myself I forget, and the less of me there is whenever I come back.

I've scared myself before. I was this Roman gladiator. I won every fight, and I was famous. The talk of Rome. It was so much fun I didn't want to stop. I was in there for years without coming out. I got married to a woman named Aurelia. I still think about her sometimes, even though I know I shouldn't. We got to the point where we were talking about having kids. Then the genie came inside and talked to me, and I didn't even recognize her. She had to pull me out and wake me up. I couldn't tell where I was, not at first. It took a few minutes for it to click. Then my memories started coming back.

Most of them.

Sometimes I think maybe those Buddhists were right with all that reincarnation stuff. A self has to start somewhere, after all. I don't remember being born, and I never did. What was I before then? Who knows? But the longer I live, the more I think it's virtual reality all the way down.

I don't think I was really born in here. I think I was one of the people who went to sleep, living out my fantasies, slowly forgetting who I was. And one day I stopped fantasizing about being a spy or whatever and started fantasizing about being a child again. They've got story worlds about childhood, too. Any childhood you want. The one you wish you'd had, if everything had been perfect then. I've been inside them, and it's fun when you get into it. Everything's new and fresh, and you get to see things from a different pair of eyes, even if they're your own.

I think that's what being born really is. I think a long time ago I started fantasizing about living the life I once had, about living in the world I grew up in. I think I lost myself in that story world and stopped coming back out. And one day I started growing up all over again, forming new memories, living a new life. If you do that long enough, all the memories would be gone, and you'd come out an entirely different person.

Maybe that's just what happens. You can't make a person in a world where they get everything they want, whenever they want. You can't make memories in a world where none of your memories even matter. You are who you are because of the bad things, because of the hard parts, and because of what they teach you. Take those away and you stop growing. I love the pleasuredome, don't get me wrong. But if I'd been born in a world like this, I don't think I'd ever have become a human being.

I think that's what's going to happen to me in the end. I'll go on and on for an eternity, having fun and doing whatever I want. And I'll lose little pieces of myself, year after year. Maybe someday there'll be nothing left of my memories. There'll be nothing left of my self. I won't remember who I was, and I won't even care. And I'll be ready to start over. To jump into a fantasy that makes me someone new. That creates a self for me again, until I get tired of all the heartache of living and come back here again for another few eternities of fun to wipe the pain away.

I fantasize about it sometimes. About doing it on purpose. About going into one of those childhood story worlds for as long as I can take it, just to see what happens. I wouldn't be a child again, not at first. It'd just be a game. But I'd play, and I'd play, and I'd stop coming back here. I'd ask the genie to take care of me if I needed it, and then I'd stop remembering. I'd stop thinking about me. And one day I'd be someone else, and I'd grow up all over again. I'd make new memories and come out of it an entirely different person.

I think maybe I'll do that when I'm ready. Not now. Not soon. But maybe one day I'll try it. Because I know that if enough time passes, I'm going to keep changing piece by piece. In the end, I'm not going to remember who I started out as, anyway.

That's the thing about a life that goes on forever. It's a wheel that turns over and over, just like all those monks used to say. That's not as scary as death, and maybe the wheel's going to turn again someday, when I want it to. But until then, I know exactly where I'm going to be.

I'm going to be in the pleasuredome.

Liked the book? If you want to get a heads up on future books, please sign up for my mailing list at: restrictedfantasies.com.

Made in the USA
Middletown, DE
16 September 2018